Terr  or

The Solution to Muslim Terror

A novel by
V. Igilante

Copyright © 2009 by Burlington National Inc.

ISBN 1-57706-653-7
ISBN 978-1-57706-653-8

The authors can be contacted at: terrorterrorterror@yahoo.com

Burlington Book Division
Burlington National Inc.
USA, Canada, England

Printed in the United States of America

10 9 8 7 6 5 4 3 2 1

Acknowledgment to the Real Authors

The author's name, V. Igilante, is obviously a pseudonym, or pen name. This book was an e-mail internet collaboration by the following authors. The authors have a wide range of backgrounds and had a great time sharing and collaborating with each other.

The order of the authors very roughly corresponds to the amount of writing or editing. The input of all the authors is greatly appreciated. We also want to thank the many authors who put time and effort into this book but, because of a fear of radical Muslims, preferred that their names not be listed. The fact that most writers did not want to have their names associated with this book because of fear of Islamic retaliation is the number one reason you will want to read it.

Two of the contributors are Muslim, but they also chose not to have their names included because of their various family connections.

List of Contributors
George Gleason; Phoenix, AZ
Roy Caldarera; Vista, CA
Alton Tubbesing; Los Angeles, CA
Jeffery Trotter; Raleigh, NC
John Larson; Yuma, AZ
Kathy Balser; Metairie, LA
Alan Clingman; Chicago, IL
Joan Goulan; Philadelphia, PA
Tony Bernanke; New York, NY
Paul Kiselar; Mesa, AZ
Donna Matthew; Pittsburg, PA
Charles Carillo; Torrance, CA
Dan Sticker; Sioux Falls, SD
Kirk Robinson; Wichita, KS
Bill Oppenheim; Manhattan Beach, CA
Robert Thibodea; New Orleans, LA
John Meckling; Portland, OR
Robert Whitten; Paradise Valley, AZ
Brian Nicholas; Van Nuys, CA
Lisa Yates; Oklahoma City, OK
Rene Sauber; Tonasket, WA

Tim Camaille; Columbia, SC
Vincent Saucedo; Fillmore, CA
Cliff Savedra; Phoenix, AZ
Don Saunee; Thousand Oaks, CA
Pat Kleinschmidt; Jackson, MS
Nick Abdalla; New York, NY
Charles Collier; Knoxville, TN
Larry Amadeo; Los Altos, CA
Bryan Zimmer; Carmel, CA
JerryThomas; Denver, CO
Cathy Nielsen; Gilbert, AZ
Thomas A. Reid; Vista, CA
Ksthryn Hothan; Sandwich, IL
Janice Bowe; Sierra Vista , AZ
Richard Bothman; Las Vegas , NV
Yvonne McLintock; Brush Prairie, WA
James Milnor; Douglasville , GA
Julie Micham; Taneyville , Mo
Dolores Kuhn; Douglasville , GA
Gary Milnor; Cantonment, FL
Marilyn Lyons; Elwood, In
James Davis; Montpelier , IN
Tracy Jeannette; Northfield, OH
Bill Manacapilli ; Universal City , Tx
Norm Whiteland; Orwell , OH
Rose Mary Porter; Commerce, TX
Jane Lemmon Elwood, In
Carolyn Hackerson, Montpelier , IN
Stephen Frederick; Trenton , MI
Pat Levely; Anaheim , CA
Adam Hewell; LaMarque , TX
Faith Conde; Crystal Falls , Mi
Samuel Andews; Tyler , TX
David Calhoun; Metairie, LA
Larry Brown; Reno , NV

Preface

The purpose of this book is to explain the truth about Islam terror in a fast-paced thriller novel. Many people who would never read a dry, non-fiction book will read a novel and thereby gain an understanding about real world facts.

This educational purpose is the prime reason so many people from around America decided to donate their time and effort to assist in the writing and the proofing of this book. We all are motivated by our beliefs that the conflict with radical Islam is one of the major challenges faced by free people everywhere.

Terror Terror Terror is available both as a free PDF Internet book and a normally priced paperback book. For more information go to: www.terrorterrorterror.com.

We believe this book will educate many people about the realities of radical Islam, and thus lead to a better understanding of how to answer their challenge.

Chapter 1

New York City
Present Time

"It was a horrible day, a really horrible day," Dr. Ralph Jackson reflected. "I was making my rounds at the hospital when a nurse told me to look at the news. At first, I thought it was an accident. Then the second plane hit. Even then, I didn't think it would affect me," he continued. "I live across town, far away from the World Trade Center.

"After my rounds, I went home and found an urgent message that said my son was there, at the Trade Center, interviewing for a job, and he was missing.

"For a long while, I hoped that he was still alive and not in the towers. I wondered whether he missed his appointment and somehow couldn't contact me. There was no way for me to find out. I lived in hell during those next two days. Then I found out that he was killed.

"The pain bent me over, and then knocked me down. It was the most horrible thing that ever happened, and I hope I never experience anything like it again. Never a single day goes by that I do not remember my son. Even though years have gone by, the feeling is still there. It will always be there."

Dr. Jackson stopped and watched the eyes of his patient, Craig Miles. After a pause, he continued, "I loved my son completely. He was a good boy. He was so good. He was my life and to have him murdered that way. The impossible happened. My world was turned upside down. My head felt ready to explode. I had the worst headaches that came from the stress and anger that the Muslim terrorists brought to me. It was too much."

"I missed him so very much. My bleak life lost all meaning and seemed hopeless. I had to take a leave of absence from the hospital. I couldn't believe this could happen to me. I will never forget. I will never forgive. Why, why, oh God, why?" asked Dr. Jackson. A depressed look came over his face and he rocked back and forth in his chair. "I am no longer a father and now I will never be a grandfather. I grieve every day of my life."

Before Craig could say anything, Dr. Jackson proceeded, "It didn't make sense. All I got was a hollow and unsatisfying answer from my minister. He said that God never gives us more pain than we can take. He said God knew I could handle it. Does that mean that Brian's death is my fault for being a strong person? I blamed myself because I was so strong that God thought I could handle it.

"After that, I left the church. They failed me in my time of need. What occurred on September 11th has changed my life forever." There was a look of sorrow and despair on Dr. Jackson's face. His eyes were wet as if he were fighting off tears.

Craig looked at Dr. Jackson and thought this was a strange way for a doctor to talk. Dr. Ralph Jackson was Craig's oncologist, treating him for cancer. All their other talks were about cancer, medication and lifestyle changes. Craig's cancer was inoperable. If Craig used the right medication and treatments, he could live perhaps a year. The end would be extremely painful and difficult. The feeling of immortality that he once had was gone. Now, he could picture his own death. It scared him to no end.

Craig had to leave his job as an airline pilot and had no real savings. He had disability income, but there were large credit card bills. He always seemed to spend everything he made. His hobbies in order of preference had been women, Jack Daniels, and gambling, mostly blackjack and roulette. His fondness for women and gambling casinos cost him a bundle, and now he was worried about making ends meet. More than worried; Craig was frightened. Craig had a family and now what? What does an unemployed, dying man do?

Craig had always known life was short, but, like most people, he lived his life as if it would never end. Like most people, he deceived himself about the truth of life and death. He occupied his mind with the umpteen million things that actually meant virtually nothing when compared with his inevitable and quickly-approaching death.

Craig wondered if he would ever understand the meanings of life and death. Was his whole life to end this way with no explanation? Was life a movie where God would not show you the last half an hour of the film? Before, Craig never thought about these things, but now they seemed to occupy all his thoughts.

"Craig," said Dr. Jackson. "We have to talk. Could you meet me for dinner later today?"

Craig was stunned. His time was running out and Dr. Jackson wanted to meet for dinner? They hadn't even discussed his condition. What could this man possibly want to discuss over dinner?

"Well, doc, I'll tell ya'. I'm a little confused. I feel bad about your son and all, but shouldn't we be discussing my situation?" asked Craig, opening his mouth for the first time since Dr. Jackson began his monologue

Dr. Jackson paused for a few seconds and looked at a picture of his son. "At dinner, I'd like to talk a little bit more about my son, but this conversation mainly concerns your condition," replied Dr. Jackson, with an expression of anxiety.

Craig tried to once again offer his sympathy concerning the terrible disaster that happened to Dr. Jackson's son, but Dr. Jackson continued to press, "Can you meet me?"

"Okay," said Craig, with a sigh and a thoughtful nod. "What time and where?"

After Craig left, Dr. Jackson continued to sit for some time, idly rapping a pencil on the top of his desk. Dr. Jackson felt a tremendous satisfaction from the events he had just set in motion. He also felt tired and, in some way, really lonely. He would have liked to have been able to talk to his murdered son and tell him that it had begun.

Chapter 2

New Orleans
Spring, 2008

As Karen Mehurin was growing up, she had a difficult time relating to her mother. Her mother had a subconscious dislike of her ever since she was born, and they became competitive for the attention of Karen's father. Karen's mother oftentimes told Karen how bad or wrong she was, but rarely praised her for the things she did correctly. Karen's father genuinely liked her, but he owned a small restaurant that required enormous amounts of his time, so he was often absent.

During her high school years, Karen was quite insecure. On the surface, she was popular with her classmates, but beneath that, Karen was shy and saw herself as very plain and dowdy looking. She attended one year of collage but lacked the financial resources to continue.

She began her career as a secretary for the Immigration and Customs Division of the Treasury Department located in the New Orleans Customs House at the foot of Canal Street. As her career started, she quickly wanted more.

Karen developed into a perfectionist and paid close attention to details. She learned how to do things and was willing to do what it took to get the results she wanted. She was good at her job, but she also knew that she would have to seize every opportunity life gave her.

In the federal government's 'GS' ranking system, the level of an employee's education was very important. A master's degree helps one obtain a better job and a lot better pay grade than a mere one year of college. The strange thing was that the degree was more important than the college one attended. Karen knew this and obtained a master's degree from an accredited mail order college. All the government seemed to care about was that it was a degree and that it was from an accredited university.

Another important thing about government work was who you knew, or in other words, politics. Karen was tall and strong, with independent manners and habits. Most people liked Karen, but that wasn't enough. She knew that in today's world, a woman could be as attractive as she chose to be, and that it behooved most women to be as attractive as possible.

First, Karen restricted her fat and food intake and lost a substantial amount of weight. She then went to a doctor who made her nose smaller, her breasts bigger and her lips fuller. Her eyes became a startling bright blue, thanks to her new tinted contact lenses. She took modeling lessons and learned makeup techniques. At a seminar on flirting she perfected a trace of a sensual come-hither look in her smile. She bought sexy cloths, a red sports car and had her hair colored blond to go with her new image. For good measure, she slept with a number of high-level managers.

Not surprisingly, Karen advanced quickly in her department and became a manager. She was very adept at using the men in her office to continue her rise but she didn't respect them. The men she met were easily manipulated and she felt superior to them. Strangely, this power led to her support of the women's movement for equal pay and treatment with men. A few years and promotions later, Karen eventually became a Treasury Agent with a GS-17 rating and received the greatly increased pay that accompanied it.

Fortunately, the Katrina flooding of 2005 did not unduly disrupt her life. Her condo close to the river was on high ground. After a short evacuation to Houston, Karen returned to her normal life.

As part of her job, Karen occasionally met Muslim women who wore the hijab, or veil. Karen heard that these women were not much better than slaves and tried to question them about their views. None of them wanted to talk about it. Karen was a government authority figure, and they probably feared her. Also, they were never alone. Often their husbands were with them. If not a husband, another person was there, so anything they said would get back to their husbands.

One day, Karen met an Arab woman with immigration issues from Lebanon who would talk. Her name was Liliane, and she was a Christian Arab. She had quite a bit to say about women's freedoms.

After Liliane's immigration problems were resolved, Karen asked, "Liliane, I am curious about the hijab. Why do Muslim women wear it?"

Liliane answered, "Because they have no choice. When you wear the hijab, you feel very small, like an unseen non-person. Still, a Muslim woman must obey her husband and also obey the Sharia religious law. There are terrible consequences for not obeying. You can be beaten or killed. Women are completely controlled and require a male guardian's permission even to get an education."

She continued, "Women are slaves in Islam, and the men have all the rights. It's hard to believe, but in an Islamic country, women are not even allowed to drive cars."

"It sure sounds like Islam is deeply antifeminist. I have noticed that many Muslim men will not shake hands with me. Why is this?" Karen asked.

Liliane's thick dark hair had fallen across one eye. She pushed it away from her face and answered, "Women are beneath them. We are not their equals and they do not treat us as equals. Sometimes it seems to me like a caste system, and we are the lowest caste, the slaves."

"What is this about polygamy?" Karen asked.

"Yes, it's true. Under Islamic law, a man can have four legal wives. If he wants a fifth, he must divorce one of the four, but that is easy. He just has to say, 'I divorce you,' three times, and he gets rid of one wife and can get another."

"An example is Abdul al-Sayeri, a Muslim who lived in my home town. He is sixty-five years old, and his desire is to marry and divorce a new woman every year, as a birthday gift to himself. Abdul al-Sayeri has married sixty-five women and can't remember most of their names. He likes to marry girls at the onset of puberty and believes that girls about thirteen years old make the best wives. He does not know how many children he has and obviously can't remember their names either."

Liliane continued, "Of course, a woman can't have more than one husband. There are all sorts of other requirements which you Westerners would not believe."

"Such as?"

"For example, a wife who refuses her husband sex whenever he wants it is considered insubordinate, and the husband has the right to physically punish her. It's really no better that being a slave. But I must go now. Perhaps I said too much. Even though I am not Muslim, all people in a Muslim country must obey the Sharia religious laws."

Karen just shook her head. "Don't they know this is the twenty-first century? Liliane, thanks for the talk. I always knew there was something wrong with those veils."

Karen now had an instinctive dislike of Muslim men and the way they took advantage of women. These poor women had none of the opportunities of free people, but Karen could not think of anything she could do to save them.

Chapter 3

New Orleans
Spring, 2008

The phone rang.

"Karen, this is a voice from your past."

Karen paused for a second. "Saleh, is that really you? I'd know your voice anywhere."

Saleh Mahfouz was one of the Treasury Agency law enforcement managers who helped Karen during her quick rise. His parents were from Saudi Arabia, but he was a moderate Muslim, born in America, who accepted people from other religions and customs.

Since 9-11, Saleh was in demand and moved on to bigger things in Washington. He did, however, spend some of his childhood years in Saudi Arabia and had a good command of the Arabic language.

"I took a new job in private industry with a very small group of people."

"Which group?" Karen asked.

"The group goes by the name 'T-3,' but, you know what they say. If I tell you any more, I'd have to shoot you. It's one of that kind of groups," Saleh responded.

It sounded intriguing already. Karen followed up, "You've taken a job with a group of people you can't talk about? Sounds very James Bond. So, are you having fun yet?"

Saleh laughed out loud at Karen's James Bond reference. "Definitely, and that's what I want to talk to you about. Can you get free for lunch tomorrow? It could be a real career advancement for you."

Career advancement? With James Bond. Now Karen's curiosity was piqued even higher. She would make herself available for lunch. "Okay. How about Mr. B's restaurant in the Quarter?"

"No, that won't work," Saleh hesitated. "We need a bit more privacy than that. Let's grab a Ferdie Special Poor Boy at Mother's Restaurant. We'll take the food down to the riverfront past the aquarium and find a bench so we can eat and have a private talk. I love early springtime in New Orleans. It has almost perfect weather. There are no hurricanes, low humidity and moderate temperature. The riverfront is a beautiful place to enjoy it. Does 11:30 sound good?"

Karen quickly agreed. She also loved the Mississippi River. It was the soul of New Orleans and the reason for its existence. The Woldenberg Riverfront Park, behind the aquarium, was a great place to observe the river and the ocean-going ships that cruise up and down it.

The next day, on the riverfront, Karen put her best sultry smile on her face and walked up to Saleh. She wasn't about to let any chance of career advancement slip through her fingers. She looked Saleh in the eyes and said, "You haven't changed a bit. It's not fair that men look young so much longer than women." Saleh glanced at his wristwatch and noticed that, as usual, she was exactly on time.

"You even look younger than I remember you," replied Saleh as he gave her cheek a slight peck. Karen smiled and thought that maybe the Retin-A cream and the Botox really did help.

"You look great yourself," replied Karen as she tossed her head slightly. Saleh didn't believe her for a moment as he was no longer in shape and his hair, what was still left, was showing ever-increasing traces of gray. Still, he wanted to believe her, and he immediately remembered how much he always liked her.

Her slim, but big-breasted, feminine shape turned him on. She was a charming woman, with sparkle and vivacity. He remembered she was really a handful in bed. He recalled the sex was especially dynamic and exhilarating, but he resolved to keep the meeting strictly business.

They found a secluded metal bench by the river and sat down. This was the busiest section of the Mississippi River since New Orleans is only about fifty miles from the Gulf of Mexico.

Large cargo boats from many countries, trains of barges filled with grain from the Mid-West, and ferry boats all took their turns on the river. The temperature was warm in this city where summer never leaves for more than a few weeks at a time. The tunes of a calliope drifted through the air from the *President*, a paddle wheel sightseeing tour boat.

"Are the Saints doing anything this year?" Saleh, once an avid football fan, asked.

Karen sighed. Why waste this time doing the small-talk routine? Saleh said he had a way for her career to advance. Karen wanted him to get right to it. "They are the same old Saints," she answered. "They have good seasons and bad seasons. They just need a little work on their offense, their defense and their special teams."

Saleh laughed, "Oh well, that's football. That's why they call it a game. Tell me what you have been working on recently."

That sounded like a subtle segue to Karen. "I just finished investigating a case for the SEC and the IRS. It seems that a number of stocks had unusually large put options just before the IRS released a very negative report on their audit. The stocks went down and a hefty profit was made on the puts. I took this electronic genius they call 'the Wiz' with me, and he discovered a very sophisticated laser listening device that was across the street from, but focused on, the IRS conference room window. Speech inside the room vibrated the glass window pane slightly, and the laser picked it up. They had a super-computer that cleaned up the vibrations and translated them into words. They knew everything that was being said in that room."

Saleh was visibly impressed. "Wow. Did you catch the bad guys?"

"Yes, we disabled the laser and just waited until someone came along to fix it."

"Greed got them again, eh?"

Karen smiled and nodded. "Yes. If they had stopped, we would have had a very difficult time tracking them down."

Saleh reminisced, "I remember 'the Wiz' from years ago. I once gave him a hard time about his beard and blue jeans not being the proper dress code. The next day, my computer went crazy. Every time I typed in the word 'the', it looked fine on the computer screen, but when I went to print it out, every 'the' was changed to 'the stupid.' Unfortunately, I did not catch it until my boss pointed it out. I looked again at my computer screen and everything looked perfect. I printed it out again and 'the stupid' was still there."

Saleh had to stop in the midst of his story and laugh. "Those remarkable geeks know exactly how all our electronics operate. After that, I quickly made friends with 'the Wiz.' I realized he was a rare free-thinker, uncontrolled by the usual bureaucratic mentality, and he could wear whatever he wanted. Wouldn't you know, all my electronics started working better? It is amazing what those geeks can do for or against you."

Karen looked at her watch. She didn't come to talk football. She sure didn't come to talk about 'the Wiz.' Her patience wearing thin, she responded, "That's him alright."

Saleh took a drink, cleared his throat and decided the ice had been broken enough. "Karen, the reason I asked for this meeting is much more serious than football. T-3 is the firm that I work for. It is a private group with no government involvement. T-3's only goal is that of fighting radical Muslim terrorists, but doing so in a somewhat unique manner. It is a very small firm, but it has a guarantee of large amounts of funding from a very wealthy person who must remain anonymous."

Karen was suddenly puzzled by what Saleh had disclosed. Stunned, she said, "But you are a Muslim. Why would you want to fight Muslims?"

Saleh paused to contemplate the wording of his response. "We don't believe these terrorists are really Muslims. Just like Hitler claimed to be a Christian, but didn't behave like one, these radicals do not behave like modern Muslims. Their fundamentalist beliefs and violent actions are giving Islam a bad reputation and hurting its cause. Before 9-11, Islam was the fastest growing major religion on Earth. Now, that Muslim growth has slowed and even Christianity is growing at a faster rate that Islam."

"Sounds intriguing. Go on."

Saleh began to feel more confident about this step in his plan. He could feel Karen being sucked in by the intrigue and promise of money. "The T-3 group," he continued, "believes that a small organization with large financial assets can do something about these terrorists and change the course of history. The firm needs someone with experience to be the lead person on certain aspects of the operation, and I suggested you." Karen leaned slightly towards Saleh thereby confirming her genuine interest.

Saleh continued reeling in the fish. "The position we want to fill is that of point person. This person will be the only contact between the operational people and me. We practice very strict security, so all contacts are determined on a need-to-know only. One cell, or part of the firm, does not know anything about other cells. One of your most important functions is to distance your operatives from my firm's leader."

"What are the dangers? Would people be shooting at me?" she asked, feeling her blood pump faster at the exciting prospect of getting out of an office and getting into the action.

Saleh laughed in response. "No. The person we want will not actually go on operations, but will set them up and supervise them until they are ready to launch. The only danger is that this is not a sanctioned operation by any government. That is why we need complete secrecy. Only one supervisor will ever meet you and know your true identity. I am that supervisor, and I am the only person from T-3 who you will ever meet."

"What does it pay?"

"Are you still a GS-17?" he asked.

"Yes."

"It pays five times your salary, plus it is only a fraction of the work and headaches. On top of that, there is a very lucrative bonus program that is rewarded based on the success of your part of the operation."

"Oh, baby," she thought. Danger, intrigue and a hefty six-figure income, this was the moment she had worked for all her career. She tried her best to play it cool. "Are you serious? Five times my salary!"

"Yes. Deadly serious," he replied.

"How long is the contract?" she asked, being nearly on the edge of her seat.

"Two years guaranteed and much longer if you are as successful as we believe you will be," Saleh replied with an overwhelming sense of confidence in Karen's decision.

"What if we win the war on terror before the two years are up?" asked Karen.

Down in his heart, Saleh wished he could be so optimistic. "So far, the number of terrorists is increasing much faster than free people can neutralize them. Unless the radical Muslim leaders have a reason to change their ways, they will continue to educate children about the glories of jihad and martyrdom. This will assure that Muslim militants will have a never-ending supply of young new terrorists."

"In some Islamic countries," he continued, "public schools use textbooks that teach the virtues of jihad, an Islamic concept of a war against non-Muslims. In addition to public schools, there are thousands of Madrassas that spread religious hate. The Madrassas are religious schools that produce about two million students a year. The Madrassas are controlled by Muslim clerics, and many of them teach jihad and religious intolerance."

"Graduates of the Madrassas are eager to travel to foreign countries, fit in with the people in these countries and, on command, give up their lives in acts of terror. They believe their participation in the jihad will earn them special places in heaven reserved for martyrs. They also believe their families will be blessed by Allah because of their martyrdom. So you see, it's not likely that the war on terror will end anytime soon."

The severity and scope of this business proposition became more and more apparent to Karen. What started out sounding like a normal business proposition now sounded as a history-altering event. In essence, Saleh was asking her to become a general in the war against terror. "What would I be doing?" inquired Karen with a decreased level of confidence.

"Obviously I cannot tell you yet, since you have not committed to work with us. But I can assure you it would be something that could easily change the world forever. But once you know what we are up to, you must keep it strictly to yourself. You remember the maxims of your famous Louisiana politician Earl Long, don't you? Don't write anything you can phone. Don't phone anything you can talk. Don't talk anything you can whisper. Don't whisper anything you can smile. Don't smile anything you can nod. Don't nod anything you can wink. It will be the same for us."

"We have examined the terrorist's vulnerabilities and have a plan of attack. It is an elegant plan that is designed to turn the world upside down and make the impossible possible. It will be something you wouldn't be able to talk about, but you would be very proud of what you did. Will you need some time to think about the offer?"

Karen seemed to hesitate for a long while. The worry lines on her brow deepened as she weighed her options. Finally, she responded, "No. I will do it. I know you and trust you, and it sounds like I might actually be able to do some good against the radical Muslim terrorists. When do I start?"

Saleh smiled once again. This portion of his mission had been accomplished. "Great, we have an agreement. Give the government a two-week notice, and you will start the next day."

Saleh went on to explain that his T-3 group realized that the government was no more likely to win a war on terrorism than they were to win the war on drugs. "The thing that both terror and drugs have in common is that the enemy is not considered a nation or country. It is some elusive group of bad people," he explained.

"Rounding up drug lords and drug pushers and throwing them in jail doesn't work. There is an endless supply of people willing to take their places and earn those big bucks. It's the same endless supply with terrorists."

"Killing terrorists is not the answer," Saleh expounded. "For every terrorist the government kills, ten more are produced. It is like trying to kill roaches with a hammer. They keep breeding in the walls. You have to get them where they breed. You have to spray and destroy their breeding grounds."

"We have studied the terrorists and their breeding grounds. We know that our reasoning is sound and that our plans will work."

"Since the American government is ineffective with this new threat to freedom, a small group of patriots and I have decided to do something that will solve the problem."

After drinking in Saleh's theories and ideas with a newfound enthusiasm, Karen asked, "Saleh, now that I am on the team, tell me more about this T-3 group."

Saleh laughed, "One of the things I like about you is that you never give up. When religious intolerance raised its ugly head and targeted innocent civilians, people got upset. Some of those people have money and power. I don't know that much about the group, and I, myself, have only one contact. But just let me repeat–they are people with a lot of money and power."

Chapter 4

New York City
Present Time

"They have great food here," said Dr. Jackson. "I recommend their parcel of salmon with lobster, and they also have a great house salad."

Dr. Jackson's favorite Upper East Side restaurant was Kings' Carriage House, on 82nd Street near 3rd Avenue. It was modeled after an old Irish manor house and filled with classic furniture and turn-of-the-century antiques.

"Well, I'm a steak and potato man, and I don't eat vegetables or salads," replied Craig. "I think I'll try their grilled filet mignon with Stilton Cream sauce."

"You never eat vegetables or salads?" asked Dr. Jackson.

"No, I just don't like them," Craig responded.

"Maybe that's why," Dr. Jackson retorted with an unusually sarcastic tone.

Craig looked quizzically at the doctor and asked, "Why what?"

"Oh, nothing," said Dr. Jackson. He always wondered about people who didn't eat vegetables and somehow thought that matters such as healthy food and proper nutrition were unimportant. Dr. Jackson ordered the salmon, vegetables and salad.

They then ordered drinks and mushrooms stuffed with crabmeat appetizers. Dr. Jackson looked around as if he feared that someone was close enough to overhear them. Satisfied there was no one listening, he smiled and asked Craig if he knew why the Trade Center was destroyed.

Just as Craig had feared, Dr. Jackson was still harping on about the World Trade Center. Craig couldn't help but be sympathetic for the doctor, having lost his son, but he wondered if the doctor had forgotten about his little issue—incurable cancer. Hoping to deflect the topic for good, Craig answered, "Well, just a few dangerous crazies, I guess."

"Please." Dr. Jackson replied with a visibly annoyed tone as his face scrunched up like he smelled something bad. He shook his head, took a long swig of his Crown Royal Scotch and said, "It's a lot more complicated than that. Muslims began their war against us Christians, and all other religions, some 1400 years ago, and the war has continued ever since."

Coming to grips with the fact the doctor wasn't going to let this topic go, and that he might as well enjoy an otherwise good dinner, Craig gave up and asked, "Well, President Bush said the terrorists were just some lunatic fringe from Afghanistan or Iraq, didn't he?"

"Yes, he said that, but there are too many of them to be called a lunatic fringe. They are the mainstream Muslim fanatics, and there are many millions of them. The President was trying to be politically correct and thought the American public couldn't take the truth. He was afraid a more truthful answer would lead to mosques being set ablaze in America and many Muslims attacked on American streets."

Dr. Jackson could tell that educating Craig would be a tedious process. Still, they were sitting in a public restaurant, and Dr. Jackson decided that this was not the best place to go into great detail. Today's was their first 'social' meeting—the opportunity to feel each other out and develop mutual understanding. The next meeting would be at a more private location. Still, a harmless history lesson about the beginnings of Islam would be in order.

Dr. Jackson smoothly broke the short silence, "I want to explain 9-11 to you. Of course you know that on 9-11, Arabs came to America looking for excitement and Islamic martyrdom. As you also know, they found it. But I need to explain where this Islamic martyrdom stuff came from."

Dr. Jackson spoke fast, running sentences together, as if he was so immersed in the Islamic story that he was really eager to tell someone about it. "Islam came from a man named Muhammad. He was an ordinary sort and was born about 570 A.D. in Mecca, which is now in Saudi Arabia. By the time he was six, both his parents had died. He came to live with his uncle, who gave him a job as a camel driver. Thus, Muhammad took trips to what's now known as Syria and surrounding areas.

"When Muhammad was 25, Mecca was in jeopardy from attacking Ethiopians. Muhammad's uncle enlisted him in the small army that was to defend Mecca, but Muhammad did not like combat and ran away. For this cowardly behavior, he was ridiculed and ostracized by many in Mecca. Some say that this experience is what made him vicious in later years. When he finally got into a position of power, he personally ordered people brutally tortured and executed."

"He sure doesn't sound like a 'Jesus' type," remarked Craig.

Dr. Jackson nodded, "There is absolutely no similarity. Muhammad then became a shepherd but made a very poor living. Soon, he went to a nearby town and courted and married a wealthy woman who was about 15 years older than he. He was criticized for marrying wealth instead of earning it, but for the next 16 years, he prospered.

"Muhammad liked solitude and spent a great deal of time by himself, often going to the caves near Mecca. When he was about 40 years old, he hit upon a way to get more power. He claimed to hear messages from an angel. He said that the angel told him that he, Muhammad, was the messenger of God. The voices continued over the next twenty-three years. Today we would call him schizophrenic and send him to a shrink, but in those days, a few people began to believe him. The messages from this angel were repeated by Muhammad and written down by his friends."

Craig cleared his throat and replied, "One of the airline flight attendants claims that she heard voices from a spirit angel and could channel those voices. She even wrote down what the spirit said and let the other flight attendants read it. Is that the same kind of thing?"

Dr. Jackson smiled and agreed with a nod. "Yes, but in today's world, people don't think all voices come from God. In fact, some people who practice devil worship say that they hear voices. Fourteen hundred years ago people were much more superstitious. Back then, people were more willing to believe every voice that came from an unidentified source was the voice of God. There were people who wanted to believe that Muhammad was giving them the words of God."

Dr. Jackson continued, "Within a few years, Muhammad had a few dozen followers who believed the passages he recited came from an angel of God. Naturally, the established authorities in the Mecca area refuted his preaching. They said the messages were not the word of an angel of God because the identity of the two speakers, God and Muhammad, were frequently confused. Eventually, Muhammad was driven from town, and he retreated back to the caves in the nearby hills."

"Most of the people of Mecca, even of his own tribe, hated and rejected Muhammad. When he was 52, the authorities in Mecca finally had enough of him and were getting ready to crack down on Muhammad and perhaps kill him. Muhammad heard about the threats and decided to run away. He took some of his followers and ran south to the city of Medina, which is about two hundred miles away."

"In Medina, Muhammad did much better with the local people than he did in Mecca. His personal history was not so well-known, so he attracted more converts and raised an army. Within a few years, his army defeated all opposition, and he became the leader of Medina. With the reins of both secular and spiritual control in his hands, he had absolute power in Medina. He retained his power by having all opposition brutally beheaded." As he spoke, he removed his glasses and wiped them violently with the napkin, gripping them tightly as if this helped control his anger.

Craig's eyes widened and he exclaimed, "Did you say that he had people beheaded? That's unbelievable!"

"Yes, he was as devoid of humanity as a cold steel sculpture, but it didn't stop there. Muhammad wanted to settle scores in his hometown of Mecca.

"In March, 624 A.D., Muhammad and his men ambushed a caravan returning to Mecca, which passed only sixty miles from Medina. They quickly defeated Abu Sufyan and his merchants from Mecca. Muhammad ordered some of the captured merchants beheaded and some held for ransom. Large ransoms were paid and the money helped Muhammad build a big and loyal army."

"Five years later, Muhammad was victorious, defeating the Meccan army and capturing Mecca. Muhammad rejoiced when the head of the Meccan leader was chopped off and given to him."

"Muhammad marched into Mecca and resolved some old feuds, beheading those he especially disliked. The stark options for those in Mecca were to follow Muhammad, leave town, or die. Most chose to follow Muhammad rather than move to some unknown city. During the next few years, more than 900 men in Medina and Mecca were decapitated. Unbelievably, even to this day, only Muslims are allowed to live in or even visit the city of Mecca."

"He sounds like a nasty and vicious man," said Craig as he devoured his steak. "Is that why the Muslim terrorists are so nasty?"

"Yes, it all starts with the leader. And it continues today. Did you know that only Muslims are allowed to have Saudi citizenship?"

Craig shook his head in amazement, "What if a tourist likes Saudi Arabia and wants to stay?"

"Well, that's not a problem because tourists that are non-Muslims are not allowed to even visit Saudi Arabia. Basically, if you are not a Muslim, you don't get in. The only infidels are workers, some foreign military to protect them, and foreign diplomats. It's a really closed society.

"Getting back to Muhammad, by the age of 60, he became the supreme ruler and dominated all his subjects. He took a couple dozen wives and the youngest was, unbelievably, six years old."

"Did you say six years old?" asked Craig as he shook his head. "That's only a baby!"

"Yes, six. He liked them young."

"But that was a different time. Weren't young wives more common fifteen centuries ago? Didn't everyone marry at a very early age?"

"Yes, but the problem is that the fundamentalists are still living in the past. Anyway, getting back to his story, after he turned 63, he became very sick and died of a high fever. After Muhammad's death his transcripts were put together by his followers and are now know as the Koran. The basic tenant of these writings was that Muhammad alone was the recipient of God's final message. He said that he was last of a long line of prophets that included Moses and Jesus and that he was the final messenger. Because he is the final messenger, he said that he and he alone was the 'Seal of the Prophets.' Muhammad said that his writings were the only correct word of God. Everything before him was flawed and everything that would ever come after him would also be flawed. Muhammad said Jesus was not the Son of God and that Jesus was only a prophet, and not a perfect one at that. Muhammad said he was the only perfect prophet."

"So he said that everyone but him is wrong?" Craig rolled his eyes as if to say he couldn't believe it.

"Yes," said Dr. Jackson nodding. "Everyone but Muhammad is wrong. He basically said that he is the only one who ever correctly heard God, and no one else has, or ever would, hear God correctly. He also said that he is the only one who knows how to live life correctly. By his actions, he showed that no crime was too terrible if it furthered the cause of his Islamic philosophy."

"I don't get how a man like that could have started a religion," remarked Craig.

"You're right. Islam is not a religion like Christianity and other typical religions. Islam is a total governmental, political and social system that includes religion. In Islam, there is no separation of church and state. Islam does not separate politics from religion. They are part of the same feudal system.

"This collection of Muhammad words were made into a book called the Koran. Most Muslims believe the Koran to be God's own words. Any interpretation of the Koran that differs from fundamentalism results in a sentence of death for the transgressor. There is no freedom in Muslim countries."

"But don't Muslims have constitutional rights that prevent this? And what do you mean by saying that Muslim countries have no freedom?"

"Christianity went through the dark ages. That was many hundreds of years ago, and everything has changed. Islam is still in the dark ages. Even today, Saudi Arabia has no written constitution. Sharia is the law of the country. Sharia is the Koran plus the Sunna, which is additional commentary on the Koran. Religious teachers, known as the ulama, are responsible for interpreting the Sharia and ensuring that Saudis follow their rules. An Islamic police force, whose patrolmen are called the mutawwiin, helps enforce the rules of behavior. For example, the mutawwiin makes sure that shops are closed for prayer times and that people are properly dressed and act in the correct manner. If you don't obey, the consequences are very grim.

"Even if you are not a Muslim, they will kill you for not obeying their beliefs. Almost all terrorists are radical Muslims. Almost all of those who commit suicide bombings against buses, airplanes, schools, children, and innocent civilians are radical Muslims. Almost all of those who are responsible for kidnapping, beheading and other brutality, all over the world, are radical Muslims. Muslim fundamentalism is synonymous with blood and slaughter and inhumanity to man."

"Is it just a matter of different customs?"

"It may be too much to expect people to politely accept different customs and conduct. It's natural to resist. It's not natural, however, to go to New York City and kill innocent civilians because you disagree with their customs. This is not only unnatural, it is downright evil. It's not like a real human being could purposely kill three thousand innocent human beings. Only monsters could do that. Only monsters!"

"I heard some Muslim leader say that the problem is injustice to Muslims. He said that curing this injustice is the only way to stop Muslim terror."

"Islam believes it can start wars, and when free people fight back or recover the lands from which they were driven, they call it injustice. Muslims killed most of the Christians and destroyed churches in the holy land. When the crusaders tried to reclaim the lands of religious significance from the Muslim invaders, the Muslims called it injustice. Muslim fundamentalists tried to destroy Israel and want to drive the Jews from their own land that God gave to Moses. When Israel fights back, they call it injustice. Anytime Muslims do not win a war that they have started, they call it injustice."

"These animals were able to murder my son without remorse. No act of brutality is too much if it advances their cause. They have even killed children and babies and are proud of it."

"You can only judge a people by the fruit they produce. From what I see, the fruit of the cold and uncaring behaviors of the radical followers of Islam show they are as merciless and cruel as the devil himself. Well, I have to tell you that cruel and brutal people, who start wars, behead innocent people, and purposely kill children, deserve absolutely everything they get in repayment."

Craig didn't know what to say to that last anti-Muslim tirade. He was tired of this conversation and glanced down at his watch. "Well, Dr. Jackson, this is all very enlightening and very interesting, but what do you really have on your mind?"

"I'll tell you more at our next meeting. Could you come by my office this Saturday afternoon? No one will be there, and we can have a more private talk. It's really very important that you come."

"What time?"

"Three works for me."

"Saturday at three it is," said Craig as they finished dinner.

Chapter 5

New York City
Present Time

A few minutes before ten p.m., Dr. Jackson unlocked the front door to his condo and turned on the lights. His condo was a three-story building in a row of other three-story buildings that were all about fifty years old.

Dr. Jackson went straight to the special cell phone that Karen Mehurin had given him and phoned her. "So far so good," said Dr. Jackson. "I'm really positive about his prospects for joining us." Since cell phones are routinely monitored by various government organizations, these phones were bought with phony identification. However, all involved with the operation knew to keep all conversations generic.

"When's your next meeting?" asked Karen.

"This Saturday at three. I will be alone with him and can ask the hard questions. We will be able to find out if he will do it."

Karen smiled to herself, but was silent a few moments. She then said, "Remember to take it slowly. If he won't join our group, the less he knows, the better."

"Okay. I'll call after our talk," replied Dr. Jackson

Karen hung up and put on her reading glasses that dangled from her neck on a dark blue cord. She pressed a button on her computer to deactivate the screen saver and went back to her research on the Internet. It was surprising how much information one can get on line. Of course, it didn't compare to the 'big brother' computer that Karen used in her previous job with the government, but with a lot more effort, her home computer worked wonders. Additionally, Karen still had favors she could call in from her days at the agency. But even with that, she had to be careful since she didn't want to make anyone suspicious of the new venture.

A different cell phone rang. It was her red phone, and Karen answered in French. "Major Sevorov, have you found someone?" Sevorov spoke no English, and Karen could not speak much Russian. Fortunately, both Sevorov and Karen were proficient in French.

"I think I met just the right person. He is ex-military like me and needs the money."

"Very good, but make sure you check him out one hundred percent. We absolutely don't need any surprises," Karen responded to Sevorov's good news.

"I've already started that, and I'll e-mail you the results in a week or so. Use your fifth chapter crypto decipher key code to read it," the former military officer instructed.

Karen cautioned, "Don't worry about wasting money on the investigation. We will reimburse all your expenses. Don't worry about anything except being absolutely sure he is completely clean."

Receiving the authorization he needed, Sevorov concluded, "You can count on it."

"I'll look for your e-mail."

Karen has an uneasy feeling about Sevorov. She knew he was an enforcer for the Russian mafia. She also knew that he was an ex-Russian Spetsnaz officer. Spetsnaz was an organization renowned for its brutality. She also heard Sevorov was in trouble with a high ranking mafia chief who was believed to be an ex-Soviet Army and ex-KGB officer. Still, there was nothing she could do about that situation, so she took three Di-Gels to calm her stomach, gulping them down with a glass of Diet Coke.

Chapter 6

New York City
Present Time

Craig Miles was the first grandchild on both sides of his family and had been treated like royalty. When he was two, his sister was born, and she was showered by attention, especially from his mother. It seemed to Craig that he was completely cut off from his mother's sweetness, love and attention. It was very painful for Craig, and it had a major influence on the rest of his life. Ever since his loss of royalty, he tried to avoid painful situations by running away from them and pretending that everything was all right. After graduating from college, he joined the Air Force and became a professional pilot.

Craig had a very broad range of interests and associated with separate sets of friends and circles of people who did not necessarily mix. For Craig though, the groups all fit together and made sense within his concept of his own personality. Craig's goal was to enjoy life and not suffer like he did when he lost his royal position. Not suffering was the key to his personality. His illness threw him for a loop because it brought back suffering. He was confused and in denial.

It was Saturday and Craig parked his car and walked into the three-story doctor's building. Recently, doctors and hospitals seemed to be his main destination. He entered the elevator and pushed the button for the 2nd floor.

The elevator doors opened, he entered a cream-walled corridor, and walked down to the mahogany office door. Dr. Jackson was one of those old-fashioned physicians who kept an office where he would discuss his diagnosis with the patient. Craig didn't like Dr. Jackson's office. It was where he found out he had cancer, and very little in the office had changed since then.

The office seemed very gloomy. The light was dim and had a yellowish cast that looked rather seedy instead of being a successful doctor's office. The walls were light brown and the wooden floor was polished and bare. There was a musty smell in the office that reminded Craig of the odor of old homes. The room depressed Craig, but he managed to fake a smile.

Except for one yellow flag and the normal medical diplomas, the only picture on the wall was of Dr. Jackson and his son on one of their happier days. The yellow flag was most unusual. It had a picture of a coiled brown rattlesnake on a yellow background. The words under the flag read, "Don't tread on me." Craig thought he remembered this flag from some American history book, but he couldn't recall the details.

"Thanks for being prompt," said Dr. Jackson as they shook hands. "Would you care for some coffee?"

Craig nodded his head, "Black, please."

A bookshelf was on Craig's right, so he turned his head slightly to glance at the titles on the book spines. As he expected, they were all medical books.

Dr. Jackson walked over to a small table in the far corner that had a Krups coffee maker with a freshly made pot of coffee. He poured coffee into two black coffee mugs that said, "*We Will Never Forget*", and handed one to Craig. He also handed Craig a basket filled with very fresh croissants, and Craig happily took one.

"Sit down here," Dr. Jackson said, removing a stack of papers and medical books from the aged brown Windsor chair next to his desk. Craig sat down, leaned back and ran a hand through his quickly disappearing hair. He settled into the comfortable chair and continued to survey the somewhat strange room.

Dr. Jackson had a strange smile on his face as he sat down on the sofa across from Craig. "I always thought there were no evil religions. But then those scumbags took my son. I wanted to know why. There must be reasons. So I studied Islam, and what I found really surprised me."

Craig had had enough. He stopped Dr. Jackson in mid-thought and demanded, "Okay, Doc. Listen. In case you have forgotten, I'm here because I'm dying of cancer. I appreciate your situation with your son and am, indeed, truly sorry. I just want to know what's going to happen with my cancer. Can we stay focused here?"

Dr. Jackson remained calm, not even slightly taken aback by Craig's uncharacteristic outburst. He understood Craig's apprehension about his condition. On many levels, he even counted on it.

Dr. Jackson reassured him, "Craig, I know these conversations have been a little unorthodox..."

"Unorthodox?" Craig countered.

"Unorthodox. But, while I thank you for your indulgence to this point, I have to assure you that all of this ties in with your situation right now. I just ask you bear with me for about twenty more minutes, because this topic, believe it or not, may very well change your life and, perhaps more importantly, the lives of your family."

Craig gave Dr. Jackson a frustrated look, sat back in his chair and acquiesced, "Alright. I'll give you fifteen minutes to somehow make this relevant to me. After that, I leave and find another doctor."

Dr. Jackson responded, "Fair enough. As I was saying, Islam is the opposite of freedom or God. Its goal is complete world domination. Islam is a false religion. It is a totalitarian ideology. The word Islam even means 'submission.' The whole concept of a free and lasting Islamic democracy is impossible. Any Islamic country that is somehow given democracy will inevitably revert to an Islamic state."

"Okay, I'll bite. If these countries adopt democracy, can't they just learn how to have a separation of church and state?" asked Craig with a puzzled look on his face.

"It would never work. To western, civilized minds, the idea of the Holy Mosques serving as a base for terrorist operations must be full of incongruities."

Dr. Jackson got up and walked to the corner behind his desk. He picked up a wooden cane and came back to his chair. He put the cane on his desk with the tip pointing towards Craig.

"Let me show you what I mean. I just placed a regular straight walking cane on the table. Now, with your eye on the level of the table, look at it end-ways. You see nothing but a small one-inch tip."

Dr. Jackson turned the cane ninety degrees, so that Craig could see the entire cane. "Now, when I move the cane so that you can look at it side-ways, you see the whole three-foot length of it. At first, you only saw just the tip of the iceberg. It is the same situation with Islam. Religion is just the tip of Islam, but the ideology that controls all aspects of life is the whole cane. That Islamic ideology refuses to exist with concepts such as freedom and democracy."

Dr. Jackson put his feet up on the coffee table and stretched his right arm across the back of the sofa. "Christianity separates religion from the affairs of government. Jesus said, 'Render unto Caesar the things which are Caesar's, and unto God the things which are God's.' Muhammad taught that there is no Caesar, but only Islam. He said all law should come from the concept of what was written in his Koran. He said that religion and the law were one, and there was no separation of church and state. Today, the notion of something unconnected to religious authority is foreign to Muslim thinking. The use of political and military power by Islamic clergy is considered perfectly normal." "9-11 was the largest terrorist attack in American history. On top of that, it was an unprovoked sneak attack against civilians. When the news of 9-11 came out, most Muslims, who otherwise could be considered moderate, excused the actions of the Muslim fundamentalists, or at the least they kept silent. I have never heard of one high-ranking Muslim cleric or spokesman who apologized for the Trade Center killings. There is, however, plenty of film footage of Muslims dancing in the streets and handing out candy to their kids after America was attacked. They saw this slaughter of innocent civilians as a sort of come-uppance that infidels deserved. They have no compassion for my son who they killed in their moment of glee."

Craig finished his coffee. He stared again at the strange yellow flag with the coiled snake hanging on the wall before answering. "Yeah, I saw that video, too. I couldn't understand it."

"We can't understand it because Americans do not understand Islam. We thought Islam was a benign religion with a goal of bringing people closer to God. We thought it was like all the other religions of the world. Instead, it's not really a religion. It's a government that wants to bury us. The Nazis or communists had nothing on Islam. The Muslim fundamentalists want to destroy or assimilate us. That's what killed my son. Those damned retards killed my son, and they think they will go to paradise and marry seventy-two obedient virgins. My son never hurt anyone in his whole life, and these rag heads come to my city, kill my innocent son and think they will have virgins lining up for them. If there is a just God, and I think there is, those terrorists will burn in hell."

"If some Korean communists committed mass murder in America, we would quickly punish Korean communists. But when Muslim terrorists do it, we somehow think that we have to catch and punish only those individual guilty people instead of the regime that sent them. In our minds, we see Islam as a religion instead of the political party that it actually is. Islam is part religion, but it is more political."

"Who could look at the religious cleansing and genocide in Chad without feeling a sense of repulsion against the Muslim fundamentalists who perpetrated this Holocaust? Muslim fundamentalists have traveled to Chad from various Arab countries. They converged on the areas populated by blacks and destroyed everything in sight. In some areas all that is left is decomposing human flesh from the executed black civilians. Justice for blacks in Chad requires nothing less than war on all Muslim fundamentalists."

Craig shook his head, sank back down on to his hard chair and said, "But if we bring the terrorist leaders to justice, the followers wouldn't know what to do without their leadership."

"No," Dr. Jackson said with a thin smile. "John Gordon, the former head of the White House Office for Combating Terrorism, said that Islamic Jihad metastasized into a lot of little cancers in a lot of different countries. He said that they formed groups operating under the terms of a movement that doesn't have to rely on al-Qaeda, Hamas, or any other terror group for funding, training, or authority."

"General Wayne Downing said that this is not a war. He said that what we're faced with is an Islamic insurgency that is spreading throughout the world, and not just the Islamic world. Today, there are more Muslim terrorists than there were before 9-11. So you see, just killing a few terrorist leaders is not the answer. The solution is something much more encompassing."

"The three most important things a Muslim can do are recite their dogmatic beliefs, participate in the holy war, and take a pilgrimage to Mecca. What if we stopped them from doing some of these things? Wouldn't they stop their terrorist attacks to be able to do their important things?"

"I am not sure I understand," said Craig, caught slightly off guard by the direction of the talk. "Why are you telling me all this?"

"Suppose some group killed your son and then the government set up a fund that gave you over two million dollars for your loss. What would you do with that money? That terrorist group is still out there and they are planning to kill other people's sons." Craig listened with his mouth open. He didn't know how to answer Dr. Jackson, or even if he should.

"Would you take that money and go on a long vacation? Would you buy a big home and try to forget your son? Or would you use that money to terrorize the terrorists? That's what I decided to do, and I need your help." Craig looked startled and closed his mouth, but said nothing.

Dr. Jackson went on, "We are not going to take it anymore. I will use that money to put an end to terror! I will give that money to you." Dr. Jackson paused as he noticed Craig's surprised expression.

Craig jumped out of his chair and was stunned. "What do you mean?"

"I will see that your wife and kids get two million dollars. That will easily pay off your home mortgage, your credit cards, and still have plenty of money to see your children through college and your wife through her old age. Two million cash, no income tax and all you have to do is pilot a plane one last time."

A sickening feeling engulfed Craig's stomach. "What's the catch?"

Dr. Jackson's voice was compassionate as he said, "You will die." The words seemed to stop time, and it took a moment before Craig could process them.

"You will die, but you don't have long to live anyway. Your cancer is incurable. You can skip all that pain and suffering at the end of your life. Also, you will be doing something for your family and for your country."

Craig sat down once again and leaned forward, his total attention belonging to Dr. Jackson. He now sat literally on the edge of his chair. It all seemed too fantastic to be true.

"Fate has chosen you for this great mission," Dr. Jackson smiled. "This is your moment, your destiny. You can turn your negative final months into a positive victory for yourself and for free people everywhere."

Craig sat in silence for almost a minute and knew that Dr. Jackson was waiting for an answer. He cleared his throat and swallowed hard so that he could speak. "Dr. Jackson, I hate to disappoint you, but I'm no James Bond or anything like that."

"You won't have to do any fighting or spying. Like I said, all you have to do is pilot a plane one last time. Other people will do the fighting and spying. What do you say?"

Craig hesitated for some time, starring vacantly at the wall with the flag that read "Don't tread on me," while turning the matter over in his head. The choice was between a slow, painful, agonizing death, and a quick, violent death. Craig had to make the best decision, not only for himself, but also for his family.

Finally he swallowed hard, wiped at his mouth and said, "Are you serious, messing with me, crazy, or all of the above?"

Dr. Jackson assured him, "Craig. Pardon my language, but I'm deadly serious."

Craig replied, "Wow! I don't know what to say. No sane man chooses death, and I am definitely sane. But death will choose me soon anyway. I just don't know."

"In addition to solving your personal problems, you will have a place in history. You have an opportunity to literally change the world for the better. You can help make the world a safer place," Dr. Jackson said with a thoughtful smile. "Your children will live in a much better world than the one either of us knew."

Dr. Jackson saw a look of bewilderment in Craig's eyes. He understood the immensity of the decision Craig would have to make, and that told him to go slow. "You don't have to answer me now. Take a day or two to think about it. But the prime directive in this operation is silence. So please, don't tell anyone, not even your wife. For obvious reasons, this must be kept a complete secret!"

"I won't, don't worry, and I will think and get back to you." Craig stood and shook hands with Dr. Jackson. He left in a daze, closing the door behind him.

Chapter 7

Chechnya Russia
1995

The sky was low and gray with billowing thick clouds of smoke and gusts of flame leaping and flashing above the city. It really wasn't much longer a city in any genuine sense of the word. Much of what had once been buildings and houses were now mere heaps of burning wood, bricks and concrete rubble. It stood desolate and inhospitable in its mute protest against the storm of war that the radical Muslim leaders had launched in their desire for a Muslim-controlled country.

Grozny, the capital of Chechnya, was in Southeast Russia, in the northern foothills of the Greater Caucasus Mountains. In 1995, Major Sevorov and multitudes of Russian troops arrived to regain control of several disputed areas, but Chechen Muslim guerrillas still controlled many of the mountainous strongholds in the south.

Major Sevorov was a member of the Russian Spetsnaz. Spetsnaz is short for Spetsialnoye Nazranie, which translates to troops of special purpose or 'The Special Forces.' They were a highly trained, fiercely proud unit with expertise in operations behind enemy lines. Major Sevorov was the leader of the small Spetsnaz contingent in Chechnya.

Major Sevorov attained the height of six feet when he was fourteen years old, and he continued to grow until he was six foot five inches tall, about two hundred and seventy-five pounds and very intimidating.

Because of his large size and leadership qualities, the Soviet military selected him to be an officer in the army. The Soviet military also sent Sevorov to four years of college and then placed him in the army where he believed he would fulfill his destiny. He was relatively happy with his career. His big trademark grin was able to instantly transform his face to make him appear warm and genuinely friendly. His grin and positive personality helped him advance quickly to the rank of major. Major Sevorov was as solid as a rock and never showed any sign of fear. His "I can do it" attitude inspired confidence and trust from his men.

On that fateful morning, Major Sevorov sat at his desk, looking over copies of the latest intelligence reports when his phone rang. "Major Sevorov," he answered.

"Sevorov, this is General Troshev."

"Good morning, General. What can I do for you today?"

General Gennady Troshev was Major Sevorov's ultimate superior on base. The fact he was calling indicated to the major that something of major importance was up.

"We have a situation. I need you to come to my office immediately. Whatever you have going on, drop it," the general responded.

Once Major Sevorov arrived at the general's office, General Troshev motioned for him to close the door and sit.

"Major," he began, "General Svetov has been abducted, and those rag heads say they will kill him if we do not pull out of Chechnya. Of course we will not pull out."

"What do you want me to do?" the major asked.

"Get with the Federal Security Service and see if they have any information on this Abdullah Basayev character who is demanding we withdraw our troops from Chechnya. See if we can find out where they have General Svetov. Do whatever it takes, but rescue him alive if at all possible. We don't want those slime balls to cut his head off and take pictures for television."

"Yes, General," was the major's response as he rose and headed back to his office.

The Federal Security Service was the Russian name for the domestic portion of the old Soviet KGB, and they had information on just about everyone in Russia. They told Major Sevorov that Abdullah Basayev lived in the village of Vedeno. It was the administrative center of the Vedensky district and was located in the Caucasus Mountain Range about 40 miles southeast of Grozny.

That section was under terrorist control, and it was impossible to reach by vehicle. There was only one road up through those mountains, and there were too many areas that provided ideal coverage for an ambush. Major Sevorov and twenty-six of his men climbed aboard four army helicopters and prepared for the short flight to Vedeno.

Chapter 9

Chechnya Russia
1995

The first bluish-white light of dawn shone over the crest of the distant hills bringing morning to the village of Vedeno. After the Islamic prayers that start at first light, the village began its economic life at the public bazaar near the center of town. People milled around the cluttered market buying bread, fruits, vegetables, oils, and various other foods.

At first, everything seemed normal. Business was somewhat slower than usual, but that was hardly surprising. In one stall a customer haggled over the price of two chickens. After a price was agreed, he went to the corner of the stall to select the best chickens. There in the corner, dozens of chickens lay in a heap, their feet tied together, and their eyes rolling wildly.

The transaction was cut short by the sound of approaching aircraft. It was obviously not a highflying passenger jet, but the much louder sound of multiple fighter jets quickly approaching the village.

Exactly thirty-two minutes after taking off from their airstrip, the two Russian Su-25s, and one Su-24 planes swooped down, making a couple of bombing runs on a suspected rebel stronghold on the North side of the city, about a mile from the public bazaar.

The air strikes had the dual function of softening up this rebel city and keeping the defenders confused with the noise so that they would not be sure of the target when the real attack started. The real target was on the other side of town.

Four twin-rotor military transport helicopters flew in low, from the south side of the city, so as not to draw ground fire. The arrival of the army helicopters coincided with the end of the aerial bombardment. "Surround the house," shouted Major Sevorov as his Spetsnaz team jumped from the landed helicopters.

Gunfire erupted from the inside house, and the bullets hissed over their heads. There was a pause that may have been seconds, but felt like hours. Major Sevorov had hoped that they would not have to fire into the house. He wanted to free General Svetov alive, but everyone knew that this might not be possible. He felt the sweat trickling down his back as he gave the order to fire. The Russian's Kalashnikov machine guns burst into a roar of fire.

The Russian machine gun fire did not silence the house so Major Sevorov keyed his radio and shouted to the helicopter, "Pour a very short burst into the roof and the front door."

Blazing flashes of flames shot out from a short burst of the Plamya AGS-17 high-explosive 30 mm gun mounted on the helicopter door. As the burst ended, Major Sevorov gave the signal to charge through the doors.

Seconds are almost meaningless. They are such a short time, unless people are shooting at you. Then every second expands before your eyes. Each second now looks like an hour. The hands of a watch appear stationary. The only thing that seems fast is the beat of your heart.

The house was stunned with the magnitude of gunfire, and as quickly as it started, it stopped. The only sound from the house was screaming and crying. The front door of the house, torn from its hinges by the gunfire, was open and swung against the wall.

"Hands up, hands up," shouted the Russian troops as they stormed through the doorway. General Svetov was not there. A plainly dressed woman buried her stained face in her apron and wept the intense sobs of those who can hardly weep more. The rest of the dazed family of Abdullah Basayev lay on the floor with hands outstretched in surrender. The only exception was one boy who lay dead with most of his head blown away.

"Look everywhere," Major Sevorov barked to his men. He was disappointed that his mission was a failure because of bad information from the Federal Security Service. It was not Major Sevorov's fault but it would be chalked up as his failed mission.

"Where is General Svetov? "Major Sevorov demanded of his new captives.

"We don't know," was the reply from an old man who seemed to be the elder.

"All this and no prize," thought Major Sevorov. "Damn you." Spetsnaz machismo prevented him from showing his disappointment, but he was not happy. Still, it was time to get out of the city. There was no mistaking the distinctive low rhythmic whup-whup-whup sound of the helicopter rotor blades flying overhead. Soon it would draw fire from any nearby terrorists in the surrounding area.

Then, in a flash of clarity, a thought came to Major Sevorov. This was the family of a terrorist. He remembered how terrorists were treated in Lebanon some years ago. Sevorov took out his knife and cut off the testacles of the dead son. He handed them to the oldest male in the house who was probably the father and said, "You will give these to Abdullah Basayev, and if our general is not released he will receive more body parts from his entire family."

Then a terrorist darted out of a nearby house holding a rocket-propelled grenade. A few seconds later he dropped to one knee, flipped the sighting bar up, and took careful aim at the Russians. One of the Russian Spetsnazs, on guard outside, saw this and fired his AK at the terrorist. The terrorist was hit, but too late. A threadlike trail of smoke showed that the grenade was already in the air. The projectile was poorly aimed and dropped short, exploded harmlessly into the ground, but the counter attack had begun.

"Targets to the right," the Russian guard screamed. Then the distinctive report of another Muslim terrorist's AK-47 was joined by red tracers that homed in on their position. The launch of yet another rocket propelled grenade screamed at the Russians that it was way past time to get out of there. Their small numbers would be no match against the more numerous Chechnyans once they joined the battle. Retreat was not only prudent, it was the only choice.

Major Sevorov's combat helmet was gone, and his hair hung plastered in a wet mop over his ears and forehead. He blew a sharp whistle and gave a hand signal. It was the signal to retreat. A spout of brown earth and thick black smoke showed where the enemy grenade had burst slightly behind the retreating Russians.

"Hurry, hurry," shouted Major Sevorov as his eye caught the blinding flash of yet another burst, the explosion causing a thick cloud of black smoke only a few dozen yards away. A second later something shrieked hurtling down, and past him, and struck with a vicious thump into the ground. There was no time to lose. The Russian 30 mm gun on the helicopter returned a devastating fire that succeeded in temporarily suppressing the few Muslims who had just joined the battle.

The entire family, less the father, was quickly herded aboard one of the choppers. One of the daughters resisted the order to get in the chopper. Sevorov was in no mood to argue so he just shot her. She lay screaming and dying on the ground as the choppers took off towards the Russians lines, towards safety.

Back at the Russian base, Major Sevorov congratulated all his men on a job well done. Their speed and dedication resulted in no Russian causalities. Considering the ferocity of the firefight, this was almost a miracle.

Major Sevorov's spur of the moment plan worked just as perfectly as he thought it might. General Svetov was released the next day. The day after that, the Abdullah Basayev family was released. Mission accomplished. Sevorov was exhilarated and proud.

There was no way he could have known that his great success would ultimately lead to a long string of events, culminating in his own death.

Chapter 10

Chechnya Russia
1995

"Major Sevorov! General Troshev wants to see you. When shall I tell him you are coming?" inquired the general's assistant on the radio.

"I'll be there at three. What's it about?" Major Sevorov asked.

"Your last mission, and that's all I can say."

Major Sevorov smiled. He had that great feeling that comes with a job well done. He was proud that his mission saved General Svetov. He easily accomplished an almost impossible task, and there was probably a medal or even a promotion waiting for him. He washed up, put on a fresh uniform, and hitched a ride on a GAZ-3937 Vodnik truck, driving off to see the General.

Major Sevorov entered the General's office and saluted smartly, "Major Sevorov reporting as ordered."

General Gennady Troshev tapped out his cigarette on the edge of his desk and dropped it on the floor. "At ease. Sit down, Major," said the general after he returned the salute.

General Troshev was a sullen and stern old general in the tradition of the old Soviet Union. But now, he looked even more grim than usual. He sighed and shook his head sadly. "Some disturbing news has reached me this morning," he said quietly. "You really screwed up, Major."

"What?" said Major Sevorov, his proud grin quickly disappearing. He was a man who controlled his emotions even more than most Russians, but at this shocking news, his jaw dropped. He could not comprehend what the general was talking about, and he thought he was dreaming.

"Killing and mutilating that boy, Abdullah Basayev's son. Moscow found out. It's unacceptable. Moscow wants your resignation now."

Major Sevorov swallowed hard and stared at the general. He was totally stunned and looked as if someone had just slapped him in the face. He moved forward on his chair and leaned toward General Troshev. He felt as though an icy cold claw suddenly gripped his chest. "That's outrageous! I didn't do anything wrong. The boy accidentally died from a bullet wound during the firefight when we stormed the house. They were shooting back at us. He was just a casualty of war."

General Troshev shook his head sorrowfully. "The problem is not in killing the boy. Many boys have been killed in this ugly Islamic war. The problem it is in your mutilating him."

"That doesn't make sense," Major Sevorov protested. "He was already dead, and besides, there is good precedence."

"What precedence?"

"Well, in 1985, a group of Sunni Muslim terrorists called Hezbollah kidnapped four Soviet diplomats in Beirut, Lebanon, killing one. Our KGB then sent out an Alfa team that itself kidnapped some of the relatives of the Hezbollah leaders. One of the relatives was killed and his testacles were cut off and sent to the Hezbollah leader. The three hostages still held by the Hezbollah were released, unharmed the very next day."

The major continued, "The KGB learned that you have to go after the terrorist's family. Terrorists are happy to die for some brainwashed belief. They believe their families will be proud of them. They do not want to endanger their own families. Our KGB taught us that there must be direct consequences against the families. So you see, I only repeated the same actions that had already been successfully done. I did the same thing as they did."

"No, Major Sevorov, it's not the same at all. First of all, both the KGB and the U.S.S.R. legally ceased to exist on December 31, 1991, so it is not the same. Second, the Hezbollah is just a group of terrorists. They are not a country. They are just a group of criminal terrorists, so they have no Geneva Convention rights. Terrorists give no mercy and deserve none. But here in Chechnya, what we have is a civil war. Certainly there are abuses on both sides, but nothing as brazen as what you did. The two are not the same."

"But, General Troshev, you said to do whatever it takes."

"Major Sevorov, it goes without saying that I meant whatever it takes that is legal. You broke the rules. Don't try to put any of the blame on me. You should have known better."

Major Sevorov stood and began to pace restlessly. "My performance reviews have been in the top one percent ever since I joined the army. On this last mission, I successfully rescued General

Svetov. I can understand a reprimand, but to resign over such a small thing doesn't make sense."

"Major Sevorov, my hands are tied. The punishment was decided in Moscow and not by me. If this were the old Soviet Union instead of modern Russia, we wouldn't even be having this conversation. You would already just be shot or possibly imprisoned at hard labor until you died. This conversation is over. Go outside, write your letter of resignation and give it to my assistant. There is nothing else that I can do for you."

In disbelief, Major Sevorov just sat back down. Desperation, and grief displayed in his face.

"Major Sevorov! I said you are to go outside immediately. Is that clear?" General Gennady Troshev pounded his fist on the desk. "Do you understand?"

"Yes, sir," Major Sevorov said thinly. He was too stunned by General Troshev's sudden change in demeanor to argue any more. He stood to leave. His mouth was suddenly dry and his knees were weak, but he managed to get outside. He felt just like he did as a boy when his father intimidated him. He was in shock. There didn't seem to be a way out of his predicament.

He felt like he was being pushed off a cliff. On top of the cliff was his life of power, glory, and success. At the bottom of the cliff was an uncertain life of failure, torment, and despair. The worst part was that he didn't know how to keep from being pushed. It seemed like a movie that happened to another person. But, deep within himself, he knew that it was real and it was his life!

In the Russian Spetsnaz officers' boot camp, Major Sevorov was taught how to deal with adversity. You just shake your head, lift yourself up and charge the enemy again. But Major Sevorov did not know who the enemy was. He didn't know which direction to charge.

Major Sevorov was always so proud of his strength and endurance in the face of difficulty. Now, he was faced with this suggested failure and weakness within himself. Tears began to form in the corners of his eyes. He could not accept this. He didn't know what to do.

Chapter 11

Chechnya Russia
1995

For Sevorov, vodka was one of the few loyal pleasures of life. When life was difficult, he didn't just sip his vodka, he gulped it down. When he drank, the multitude of problems in the outside world disappeared. There was nothing left except the stupor of warm feelings and a deep unconscious sleep.

Sevorov woke around lunchtime. His head pounded and the muscles in his neck and back ached from the tension he still felt. He could not even begin to remember how much vodka he had drunk. He saw two empty bottles on the floor and a half-empty glass on the small table beside the bed.

The voice of General Troshev again started to reverberate through his head. "You really screwed up," Sevorov heard again and again. Even all the vodka couldn't silence it.

He staggered to the bathroom, almost tripping over a suitcase and banging his leg against a chair. He was nauseous and barely made it to the bathroom in time.

Sevorov splashed cold water on his face and wished he had some aspirin. The toilet was a mess, and the smell was overwhelming. He had obviously thrown up the previous night and missed the toilet by a good many feet.

He steadied himself and looked in the mirror. When he met his own eyes in the mirror, he realized that the man staring back at him was a stranger. His once happy eyes that usually looked back with resolve and intense clarity now stared back at him in astonishment.

Now his eyes were swollen, bloodshot and sad. His lips were pale and tightly pressed together. The long stubble of hair on his pale face covered his strong jaw and caused him to wonder for how many days he had been drunk. He cupped some water in his hands and drank.

Sevorov wiped his shaky hands down his face, as if he was trying to wash away General Troshev's words. Slowly, the fog in his mind began to lift. Cold and clammy with the smell of stale, unwashed sweat on his body, he turned to look in the mirror again. He took out his shaving kit and started making himself presentable. He tried not to look at his bloodshot eyes and, instead, concentrated on removing his short beard.

There were tears in his eyes. Yesterday, he was a major with a promising career. Today, he was nothing. With no retirement benefits or pension, he had nothing. Sevorov served time in both Afghanistan and Chechnya. He was a decorated and combat-tested officer of the elite Russian Spetsnaz, but after this, who would want him? What good was bravery and combat experience in this new Russian capitalist economy? How could he tell his wife? What would he do? Where would he go? How would he support his family?

Chapter 12

New York City
Present Time

Karen set up her new home in New York City. She didn't like the hustle and bustle, but New York was where things happened. Karen remembered how confused she was the first time she visited New York City. She was only twenty-three years old and completely lost.

She had a map in one hand and the steering wheel in the other when a New York City cop pulled her over. After the customary license examination, the cop told Karen that she was free to continue on her way but not to read the map while she was driving. That was long before the days of GPS navigation aids, and Karen wondered how she could tell which direction to drive if she didn't look at her map.

After being sure the cop was out of sight, she continued to consult her map. The lesson she learned was that some people think you should just drive until you got somewhere. But Karen wanted to get to her destination and not just somewhere. She had been looking at maps and planning for the future ever since.

On this day, Karen sat quietly in the second bedroom of her apartment that she had turned into an office. She opened her laptop computer and relaxed while it proceeded to boot up. She liked the way she fixed up her office. The lighting came only from the screen of her laptop computer and a florescent strip light hanging in the valance above her window. The heavy curtains of the room were pulled shut, and stayed that way, to insure her privacy. The florescent strip gave Karen the illusion that the window was open and the light came from outside.

Karen didn't mind computer work. Many people dislike it, but perhaps it was Karen's logical mind that allowed her to use the computer as a tool that worked for her. She worked for an hour, or more, until she was satisfied that the letter said what she wanted. Karen wanted a short break, so she reached for her cup of coffee, but her hand immediately felt that the coffee was by now quite cold. She pulled back her hand, gave up on the coffee idea and decided to begin to encrypt her work.

People who operate a business by e-mail unknowingly allow various groups such as Homeland Security, the Federal Bureau of Investigation, the Central Intelligence Agency, the Internal Revenue Service and many other private and foreign groups to view their complete messages. Anything that travels on the internet is easily viewed by a whole host of organizations.

Encryption software and other tricks help, but modern super computers have such vast powers that no one should assume their communication is one hundred percent safe. In the modern internet age, privacy in normal communication must be considered a thing of the past.

Karen had no misconceptions about safety, but she knew the secrets of fooling even Big Brother. She used a non-repeating text function to make her messages unbreakable. Code experts would opine that, with their super computers, nothing is unbreakable, but unless you know the source of the non-repeating function, the resulting code is essentially unbreakable.

She always composed her e-mails in Microsoft Word. Karen wrote seven single-spaced paragraphs that summarized their plans. There was no way anyone but Sevorov would ever see this. The last sentence told Sevorov to memorize and destroy this e-mail.

The crucial next step was to encrypt the document using a public-key encryption. This was accomplished using home computer software that scrambled the e-mail messages so they were rendered unreadable. To unscramble the e-mail, the recipient had to use the sender's passkey.

Karen used a program called PC – Encrypt. Karen preferred this program because it had a powerful encrypt strength equivalent of well over 7,500 bits.

After encrypting the message, she saved the Word program as a PDF file and reduced the file size by using the Stuffit Deluxe program. This further reduced the possibility that some government super computer would find it interesting enough to even try to decipher her message.

Next, she transferred the message to a CD. Later, she planned to go to a public computer, insert the CD and send the e-mails over the internet. There would be no IP address on the e-mail that could ever be linked back to her.

Karen's concentration was interrupted by the distinctive ring tone of her blue cell phone sitting on the table behind her. Karen knew who it was because only one person had the blue phone number.

She answered, "How did it go, Doctor Jackson?"

Dr. Jackson had been excited about making this phone call. "Karen, I think I got his attention."

Karen hated when people played games with her. She especially hated it when she wanted someone to get to the point. "And?" she asked impatiently.

"Well," Dr. Jackson began to sputter, "Normal people don't make these types of decisions that fast."

Karen had to resist the urge to call the doctor a boob. She understood his passion for the mission, but oftentimes regretted having to work with such an amateur. She answered with a sigh, "I know, but it's all coming together and soon would be a good time."

Eager to not fall out of favor with Karen, Dr. Jackson continued, "I will keep on top of it and let you know the moment he signs on."

"Did you caution him not to discuss it with anyone?" she asked, sounding almost like a mother asking her child if he had remembered to brush his teeth.

"Of course, and he agreed."

"Good work. I'll talk to you later." Karen wasn't even really sure why she said, 'good work.' It really wasn't. This piece of the puzzle needed to be in place soon, and she found herself questioning his ability to deliver.

Karen powered down the computer, finished packing her last minute things and drove to the airport. It would only be a two-day trip. The merchandise she needed could have been delivered, but then she would have needed another address. Karen also liked to do things herself when at all possible. She had a deep distrust of others, which was one of the reasons she had survived so long at the agency.

Karen's equipment source had procured some items that would be needed, and Karen wanted to inspect them first hand. She also wanted to rent an out of the way apartment that she could use as a safe house when the need arose.

Chapter 13

New York City
Present Time

First class seats on planes may generally be nicer than those in tourist class or coach, but tourist is much more low profile and anonymous. For someone in Karen's business, anonymity wasn't an option; it was a requirement. First class was an unnecessary luxury, especially for a short eight hundred mile trip.

Eventually, Karen's row was called, and she left the New York-Kennedy Airport waiting area to board her flight. The airplane was completely full, but Karen found a spot in the overhead bins for her small leather carry-on flight bag and snapped her seat belt closed. The narrow seats were uncomfortable, and a nearby baby screamed its protest, but Karen put her thoughts on a tranquil mountain creek and willed herself to relax.

Across the aisle sat a very obese man who obviously boarded early. He had raised the armrest that divided the seats because he could not fit in a standard sized seat. The unhappy man took up a seat and a half. Karen looked up and saw a woman trying to figure out how she could possibly fit in her one half of a seat. She just stood there, blocking the aisle, not knowing what to do.

The flight attendant walked over and told the woman that the flight was full, and she would just have to squeeze into the seat or take the next flight. Fortunately for the obese man, she was a thin woman and managed to just barely squeeze in. She likely had a miserable flight, but a story to tell her friends.

After takeoff, Karen loosened her seat belt, stared out the window at the quickly receding ground and thought about what she had just seen. Amazing, she thought, how people no longer stick up for their rights. The woman paid for a full seat, not a half one, and the man deserved to be treated with respect and dignity, as well.

This type of problem originated when all the airlines squeezed more seats into each row. The airlines were able to increase the total number of seats and make more money, but the seats were then narrower, and not everyone fit in them. The airlines caused the

46

problem and should automatically upgrade heavy people to first class where the seats were wider.

"That's the problem in the world today," Karen thought. "People accept all kinds of indignities, including leaders instigating terror to kill people and getting away with it."

Karen knew something was wrong with the fear of confrontation mentality she had just witnessed. Confrontation may be difficult, but capitulation without sticking up for what was right is much worse.

Once the airplane reached cruising altitude, she took out her laptop, booted up and maneuvered to the *Al Qaeda Terrorism Manual*. The Manchester Metropolitan Police found it during a search of an Al Qaeda member's home. The manual was found in a computer file labeled as "the military series" related to the "Declaration of Jihad."

Islamic governments have never and will never be established through peaceful solutions and cooperative councils. They are established as they always have been:

By pen and gun

By word and bullet

By tongue and teeth

He [the member] has to be willing to do the work and undergo martyrdom for the purpose of achieving the goal and establishing the religion of majestic Allah on earth.

About Forged Documents:

1. All documents of the undercover brother, such as identity cards and passport, should be falsified.

2. The photograph of the brother in these documents should be without a beard. It is preferable that the brother's public photograph [on these documents] be also without a beard. If he already has one [document] showing a photograph with a beard, he should replace it.

3. When using an identity document in different names, no more than one such document should be carried at one time.

4. When a brother is carrying the forged passport of a certain country, he should not travel to that country. It is easy to detect forgery at the airport, and the dialect of the brother is different from that of the people from that country.

Karen studied the manual, not for the techniques, but to judge the sophistication of the Al Qaeda operatives. So far, she was not impressed. The next section on missions looked much more interesting.

The main mission for which the Military Organization is responsible is the overthrow of the godless regimes and their replacement with an Islamic regime. Other missions consist of the following:

1. Gathering information about the enemy, the land, the installations, and the neighbors.

2. Kidnapping enemy personnel, documents, secrets, and arms.

3. Assassinating enemy personnel as well as foreign tourists.

4. Freeing the brothers who are captured by the enemy.

5. Spreading rumors and writing statements that instigate people against the enemy.

6. Blasting and destroying the places of amusement, immorality, and sin - not a vital target.

7. Blasting and destroying the embassies and attacking vital economic centers.

8. Blasting and destroying bridges leading into and out of the cities.

Karen's reading was interrupted by the plane's intercom, "We are ten minutes from Chicago's O'Hare airport. In preparation for our arrival, please raise your seat backs to the upright position." Karen powered down her laptop. She continued thinking about number five on the mission statement: spreading rumors that instigate people against the enemy. She thought she might use something like it on her next mission. Karen reset her Rolex for local time: 8:15 p.m. When the seatbelt light went off, Karen stepped in front of the obese man, who struggled to get up, and deplaned.

At the Hertz rental location, Karen produced her current fake driver's license, which the employee photocopied and then stapled the copy to Karen's rental form. The clerk was happy that Karen took all of the insurance choices since, for the employee, this was like a tip. The rest of the transaction went smoothly and quickly. Karen got in her Chevy and punched her destination into the GPS system.

Karen drove slightly under the speed limit all the way to her hotel. She had two types of fake ID's. The good ID's would pass a computer inquiry. The piece of paper she used today was all show and no substance. Getting pulled over with this ID might be a problem. Still, she was in America, and because of her past work for the U.S. government, she knew she could get away with it.

One of Karen's talents was the ability to learn a foreign language thoroughly. She spoke perfect Parisian French without any

American accent. This helped her when she worked as an agent. Being an operative, however, was a young person's game and Karen was now almost forty years old. She already proved that she could play that game, and now she wanted to prove she could successfully handle the management and planning parts.

If Karen were a lesser woman, she would certainly have backed away from the history-changing task that confronted her. But she knew she could do it. She knew that now was the time that people who loved freedom needed her skills. She knew that she was perfectly trained and positioned to accomplish the mission which she had accepted.

Chapter 14

Chicago
Present Time

"Good morning, Sandy," said the owner of Stan's Imports in Chicago. That was where Karen often bought some of her hard-to-get equipment. Stan's Imports had a Class Three federal firearm dealer's license, so he was legally able to own fully automatic weapons. Also, he had the connections to obtain just about every sort of communications gear, gun, spy equipment and body armor available. Stan could even get almost any type of illegal equipment, but it cost more and was available only to his special repeat customers.

Stan's Imports knew Karen by the alias of Sandy. Karen had previously bought various guns and surveillance gear from Stan. "What can I do for you this fine morning?"

"Morning, Stan. I just came to pick up that order I phoned in."

"Oh, yes, Sandy. I have your order ready to box in the back. I will get it," Stan assured his valued customer.

Stan kept his special military items in the back where the casual shopper could not see them. In the front were just knives, swords and various other legal items. Karen looked at some of the knives until Stan returned and laid Karen's items on the counter.

Stan beamed like a father showing off his newborn son. "Sandy, what do you think of the body armor?"

Karen was genuinely impressed. "You were right, Stan. If you didn't know what to look for, this new Columbian body armor looks just like normal clothing. It looks just like real thick and warm underwear."

Stan was glad she was pleased. "Yes. It's not as effective as military armor, but it will easily stop a handgun firing hollow point ammunition. Can I interest you in any weaponry, passports, driver's licenses or any other material?"

"No, not today."

"Can I box the body armor up for you?" Stan asked.

Karen paid the bill, counting out hundred dollar bills, and drove off with the new style body armor, heading towards her next destination. She relaxed and adjusted her seat back into a more restful position. She kept her guard up, however, because she hadn't worked in law enforcement all those years without looking in her rear view mirror and paying attention to details. Karen's self-preservation instincts began to say something was wrong.

Her self-preservation instincts were right on since it appeared there was a possible tail. Karen picked up on a gray Ford sedan, parked diagonally across the street that pulled out behind her.

Karen immediately took a right turn, and the gray Ford sedan went straight, but a second car also took a right. The tail changed chase cars, but it remained just the same. Surveillance vehicles often take turns following the subject to frustrate identification of the tail. Karen took a left, but they were still there.

Karen thought this was quite odd. Why would someone possibly be following her? Karen took a right and the tail took a right. Her heart started pounding harder. There was no doubt that someone was interested.

The thought occurred to Karen that it was possible her arms dealer was under surveillance, and anyone leaving Stan's Imports was automatically followed. With this never-ending war on terror, good guys were tailing good guys. With the new national intelligence director in charge of the money, everyone was into everyone's business. Freedom from surveillance was a thing of the past. It was a mess. Good guys or bad guys, it made no difference. Tails are bad and she had to lose them, regardless of their source.

Karen slid into the stream of cars heading east and drove towards the loop in downtown Chicago. Under Michigan Avenue there were large multi-room parking garages. One of those would be an ideal place to lose a tail. Karen took the down ramp to the garage and drove south a block until she saw a spot where she could quickly back in. Her tail knew what the back of her car looked like, but not the front.

Karen lowered her head and waited while a number of cars went by. After twenty minutes, Karen thought it safe and started her car. She drove through the pay booth and everything still looked good. It would take at least thirty seconds to get through the pay booth, so if there still was a tail behind her, they would be stuck long enough for Karen to escape.

Chapter 15

Moscow, Russia
Present Time

Lieutenant Nick Sergankova was once a very low-level staff assistant to General Vladislav Schnitzer. Before he ended up in this dead end position, he had a bright future. His father had political connections, and this helped him become an officer in the elite Russian Spetsnaz. But things didn't turn out the way he envisioned. Lieutenant Sergankova tried to fit in with his class, but his personality was very flat and bland.

He was also the smallest in his training class, weighing in at a mere 165 pounds, but he was a compact, vigorous and strong man who moved with the speed and agility of a mountain cat. He was basically a loner, but he tried to overcome that personality trait. He wanted camaraderie with his class, but he didn't know how to go about getting it. The things he excelled at were not team functions. He was the best marksman in his class. That provided him some measure of status, but it didn't help in getting along with others. In the Russian Spetsnaz, as in most jobs, personality was more important than performance.

Lieutenant Sergankova never saw any combat and was soon transferred to a staff position in Moscow. Moscow was good duty, but his job was boring and every day he dreaded coming to work.

The job became so dissatisfying that when his enlistment was over he did not re-enlist. This was the new free market Russia and many of the new companies looked attractive. He landed a job with Vimpel Communications, one of the two largest cell phone companies in the Moscow area. It was just a job, but it paid better than a lieutenant's salary in the army. Nick hadn't married, but loved playing with his brother's young children on his days off. The presents he brought them required a little more disposable cash.

Then, on a fateful Wednesday in September, something happened to change Nick's life forever. He was on his way to a quiet pub where he liked to drink a few shots of vodka and relax after work. It was not very many blocks from the building he worked at, so he leisurely strolled down the street with a gait that was close to a glide. He was absent mindedly recalling his army adventures when he heard a hysterical cry for help. He looked up and less than half a block in front of him were two men. One of them slapped a young girl and dragged her by the hair. They headed for a nearby white van with an open door. Nick didn't really know what was going on, but he sensed that these men were bad guys. A sudden rage shot through Nick's body as the scene somehow reminded him of the Muslim baby killers in Beslan, Russia.

He continued walking normally towards the men and when he got within arm's length of one of them, he stopped. Nick could not explain what he did next. It may have been the scars from his military service, or it could have been that helpless frustration of working for a cell phone company while hundreds of school children were murdered by radical Muslims. He only knew he had to respond.

Abruptly, without warning, he spun his body to the left and in a blur of action, struck one of the men with the side of his right hand. It was a karate chop to the carotid artery of the neck, and the man just dropped to his knees and crumpled in a heap, out cold, face down on the sidewalk.

It happened so rapidly and so unexpectedly that it was a total surprise to everyone. There was not one word spoken as Nick just exploded into action. Nick's swift attack caused the second man to hesitate momentarily and stare at the maniac who attacked his partner. Then, the second man quickly yanked a small .380 automatic pistol from his coat pocket and shouted, "Freeze!"

A pointed gun speaks with a language that is understood by people everywhere, but each individual's reaction depends on his training. Most people in this situation would see the barrel of a gun that seems to have a diameter the size of a large cannon. They would just freeze as instructed. Other people might panic and try to think what they should do.

Nick didn't freeze and didn't think. All his being was controlled by automatic reflexes drilled into him by some of the most demanding military training in the world. His eyes observed everything with total clarity and everything seemed to happen in slow motion. Nick stopped and stood completely still, his face unemotional, and asked softly, "Hey, there. What do you want?"

For a brief moment, the man with the gun paused. His eyes widened, and he opened his mouth to start to say something. That's when Nick went into action again.

The human mind can be easily tricked. Nobody can think about more than one thing during the same exact moment. When the gunman first began to speak he thought about what he would say and what his response would be. He thought about what he would demand from this little man.

This created a very small window of opportunity for Nick. The gunman hesitated for less than a second, but it gave the edge to Nick as he went into an automatic mode of his Russian Spetsnaz martial arts training. His mind instinctively concentrated on the task at hand.

From below the gunman's field of vision, Nick's left hand came up and grabbed the gunman's right hand. Nick moved the gunman's hand over to Nick's right and away from Nick's body. At the same time, Nick turned his body clockwise to remove his body from the direction of the gun. As he did this, his right leg stepped backwards to further remove his body from the gun. These three simultaneous movements pointed the gun away from Nick and moved Nick's body even further from the direction where the gun was aimed. If the gun went off now, it would not hit Nick.

Nick's movements continued to automatically flow from his years of training. His right hand immediately came up and grabbed the barrel of the gun and forced it back towards the head of the gunman. The gunman tried to draw his hand back, but Nick now had two hands on the pistol and the gunman had only one. The gun was effectively neutralized, but Nick continued the movement.

Nick quickly repositioned his right foot behind the gunman's right foot in preparation to slam him into the ground. At the same time Nick rotated his body counter-clockwise, putting pressure on the gunman's hand. The gunman's finger that was still on the trigger was unable to dislodge itself. The gun was pointed at the gunman's own head, and because of the pressure of his own finger on the trigger, the gun fired. That was exactly the result this disarming movement was designed to do, and it worked flawlessly.

The blast of the pistol was very close to Nick's ears and was deafening. The bullet went through the gunman's head and blood splattered on Nick's face and clothes. Nick automatically completed his martial art movement and pushed the gunman to the ground. The gunman fell in front of him, lengthwise, face up, motionless, and dead.

The disarming movement was also designed for Nick to retain possession of the gun, and it also worked as planned. It was obvious that the gunman was dead, so Nick immediately pointed the gun at the other man who remained on the ground. If he made the slightest movement, Nick was trained to instantly shoot him twice. But he was still completely unconscious. It was over as suddenly as it had begun. The entire conflict took less then ten seconds from beginning to end.

A wild cry broke from the girl's lips. She stared open-mouthed at the epic that unfolded before her. So great was her emotion that she could not say the words she wanted. The girl alternated between screaming and crying, but Nick mostly just heard a ringing in his ears as a result of the close explosion of the gun.

Nick searched the man on the ground, removed a pistol from his pocket, and shouted for the people standing across the street to call the police. Someone called the police and, after what seemed like an eternity, they arrived to take control of the situation. The girl was perfectly safe, but the experience would no doubt inhabit her nightmares for years.

The unconscious man was arrested and Nick, the girl, and three witnesses were escorted to the police station for questioning. The young girl was still frightened, confused, and was not a good witness. She suffered only minor physical injuries, but the psychological injuries would surely be much greater.

Nick's attack on the gunman had been so fast and efficient that the witnesses did not know exactly what they saw. All they agreed on was that the girl was screaming for help, and one of the men was seen dragging her off until Nick saved the day.

Pravda, the Russian newspaper, had an article about how Nick Sergankova, once a lieutenant in the famed Spetsnaz, had single-handedly, and without weapons, foiled a young girl's kidnapping at the hands of two armed men known to be associated with the Russian Mafia. It said that the young girl was probably going to be used in the Mafia sex trade and that Nick was a hero. The newspaper went on to say that Nick killed one gunman and the surviving gunman's fate would be worse than death. He was certain to be given a life sentence in a Russian maximum-security prison, a place not to be confused with the country club-like atmosphere of the American federal prison system.

Nick had never before been put in a situation where he had no choice but to kill a man. In spite of his combat training, this incident would leave dreadful and depressing nightmares for a long time afterwards. He wondered how other people with his military training handled the emotional stress of their first kill.

Nick sensed that this was a turning point in his life. Indeed, it would so prove to be. About a month later, he received a phone call from Sevorov, and his life was changed forever.

"Is this Lieutenant Nick Sergankova?" Sevorov asked.

"Yes, but it hasn't been 'lieutenant' for quite a while."

"This is Major Sevorov, but as you know, it hasn't been 'major' for a long time, either." Sevorov and Nick had some minor dealings during their time in the Russian Spetsnaz.

"Hello, Major, I mean, Mr. Sevorov. What can I do for you?"

"I saw that article about you in Pravda. I didn't realize that you are no longer with Spetsnaz. I have a business proposition that might interest you. Is dinner tomorrow okay?"

Chapter 16

Moscow, Russia
Present Time

Abacus Café is a cozy little restaurant that is quite popular with the Moscow crowd. It's located on Gazetny Pereulok not far from the Central Telegraph building where Nick works. It is not very far from the clubs that shake with booming modern music, but Abacus is quieter and more civilized. It offers American, European, and Mexican cuisine, and even has American pool tables in the billiard room.

Sevorov purposely arrived at the restaurant a bit late. He didn't remember exactly what Nick looked like and was afraid he wouldn't recognize him. Nick was relatively nondescript, pretty much like his personality. Sevorov, on the other hand, stood out, and very few people who met him ever forgot him.

Sevorov walked in, looked around, and saw Nick stand up and wave.

"Sevorov! You haven't changed a bit," exclaimed Nick, even though he noticed deep worry lines that he never saw before in Sevorov's leathery face.

Sevorov laughed, "Just got more handsome, that's all. Lose that beer, Nick. Let's drink expensive vodka tonight." Sevorov ordered doubles.

"You sure seem to be in a good mood. I don't remember you ever smiling so much," noted Nick.

Sevorov took a long swig of his vodka and answered, "Instead of poverty and suffering, I now have good suits, lots of money and beautiful women. Hey, Nick, life is treating me well. I don't have those awesome responsibilities and worries that I had in the army. Now, when I do a job, I get paid very well, and then it's over. After that, I get to drink vodka, chase women, and play for a long while."

"What kind of jobs?" Nick asked out of both curiosity and envy.

"In some ways, I'm kind of a mercenary now. I work for money, and I mean a lot of money. Of course, I only accept the jobs I want, and I am always on the right side." However, Sevorov knew that this wasn't totally true since, in fact, he was associated with the

Solntsevskaya branch of the Russian mafia and often did accept somewhat questionable assignments. The Russian mafia was different than other organized crime groups in that most members and bosses were ex-military or ex-KGB. That fact made for an often more brutal mafia than organizations found in the west.

"Wow! I didn't know that," replied Nick. "Is that why you wanted to have dinner?"

Sevorov noted somewhat condescendingly, "You're quick, Nick. Tell me, are your small-arms skills still as good as when you were in the army?"

Nick was intrigued and confused. What would Sevorov want with someone like him? "Yes. I still go to the country and shoot now and then, but mainly I am a natural. As long as I can remember, I have always been shooting. When I was just a four year old, my older brother trained me to use his rifle, and I have been winning contests ever since. I think it is a family trait. It's easy for me to score on the target."

Sevorov wasn't overly concerned with Nick's life history. "Nick, I have this job opportunity, but I need a helper. After reading about you in the paper, I made inquiries. I hear you are doing something with cell phones. Are you interested in making some real money?"

As much as he hated working in the cell phone industry, Nick decided to play coy and not seem over-anxious. "I might be. What kind of job is it?"

Sevorov knew he had his prey on the hook, ready to be reeled in. "Capturing high level Arab terrorists," he replied, taking a sip of vodka. "It pays really well."

"Is it dangerous?"

Sevorov chuckled, "Come on, Nick. Life is dangerous. There are no guarantees for operations like this, but if you want to be in the game, you have to roll the dice. If we wanted a safe life, we would never have joined Spetsnaz. It sure isn't safe dealing with those murderous, baby-killing terrorists. There is always the possibility of dying, but it was the same in the army for a lot less money. Besides, we're all going to die. Do you want to live to be an old man who was never brave enough to stand up for what's right?"

Nick, slowly digesting Sevorov's arguments, nodded his head in agreement. "Ever since the 2004 Muslim terrorist slaughter in Beslan of hundreds of innocent school children, I wanted to stand up and do something. I never knew what. There is no excuse for shooting innocent children in the back. Hitler killed millions of Russians, including children. Not even Hitler went out of his way to target children like the insane Muslim fundamentalists." A look of loathing came over his face. "Then, to say you do this in the name of God, that proves that their God is really the Devil. Yes. I'm very interested. Whatever I can do to fight them, I will. But who would we be working for?"

And the trap was sprung. Sevorov responded, "You would work for me, but the people I work for are a pretty secretive bunch. You will not know who they are, nor do you need to. My employers haven't said exactly who they are even to me, but I think they're American CIA, or closely associated with the CIA. They also seem to have big-time connections in Russia. The main thing is, they are on our side in this Arab terrorist thing, and they are willing to pay a large cash advance with secured promises of the rest after the job is done."

Nick's eyes brightened, showing his intense interest. "Of course, I want to do the right thing. However, how much money are we talking about?"

People may want to do the right thing, but money is what makes the world go around. "In just a few days, you will probably make as much as you could make in ten years at the Vimpelcom cell phone company. I know it's a big decision to make without thinking about it. Unfortunately, I can only give you two days to think, and then I will have to bring the offer to someone else. It's moving very fast and I have no choice."

Sevorov thought it was a sure thing and that Nick would definitely say yes. He turned away from Nick and waved to the bartender for another round of vodka. He turned back and said, "Two days, Nick. That's all I can wait."

Chapter 17

Chicago
Present Time

One of Karen's strengths was planning a mission. She was very meticulous, and over the years learned what to do and what not to do. In this case, she would proceed as if she was never followed when she came out of Stan's Imports.

Karen's next stop was just a specialized hardware store. Over the phone, she had pre-ordered some canes made from Hickory grown in Arkansas. Hickory is the same wood that good ax handles are made from, and it is very hard and dense. The all-wood canes looked normal and could have been something an old man would use to maintain his balance while walking.

The canes were for Sevorov. He once was the technical advisor for a number of training manuals, including one called *The Russian Cane and Walking Stick as a Weapon*. The cane is just like the short staff that Sevorov learned in the weapons section of his Special Forces classes. In the right hands, a cane is a formidable weapon. A trained martial artist knows the secrets of changing an old man's cane into a weapon. Just the simple act of tightening your hand at the exact moment before the cane strikes its target greatly accelerates the tip of the cane. The accelerated cane can then inflict very substantial damage to the target.

Next, Karen stopped at a Fed-Ex store and sent the canes and the triple-extra-large body armor to herself at her New York address. She kept the smaller body armor to wear on her next flight. There was no metal in the body armor to set off the metal detectors, but like all aspects of her plan, she would personally check it out and not rely just on theory. Then it was back to the hotel to use her laptop. Karen had mail from Sevorov, and it took her a few minutes to decode it.

Nick Sergankova, the man Sevorov just investigated, had a background very similar to Sevorov. Even though Sevorov and Nick were both Spetsnaz, there were some significant differences between the men. Nick was highly trained but had no actual combat experience. Nick spoke only Russian while Sevorov also spoke French.

This meant that Sevorov could use a French passport while Nick's passport would have to be Russian. Another big difference was their weight. Sevorov was a 250 pound, six foot five inch weight lifter, while Nick was small and only 165 pounds. Karen originally wanted both men to be big, strong martial artists.

A man as big, strong, and well-trained as Sevorov was almost impossible to take down. Still, two huge men might look suspicious, and everything else appeared great. Then, of course, this was the man who Sevorov chose to be his assistant in the operation, so he would be comfortable with him.

Sevorov was actually chosen for this job by Saleh, who in turn was told to use him by a Russian Mafia leader. Whomever Sevorov chose would almost have to be acceptable. Karen sent a coded e-mail back saying that she was very pleased that Sevorov had found the right person for the job.

"If all goes successfully, I offer you each a minimum of one million American dollars. Regardless of the outcome, I guarantee $200,000 each in your numbered accounts. In the event you lose your lives in this fight for freedom, your families will get the money." Karen pushed send and was sure they would accept the offer since it was even better than she originally offered to Sevorov. There would probably be an affirmative answer the next day.

The plan was coming together even faster than Karen imagined, but she still didn't have a pilot. Karen hoped that she would get a call from New York soon.

Rain pelted the windows and thunder rumbled. It reminded her of the rainstorms in her childhood while living in New Orleans. Those were the peaceful days before she joined the agency. For some minutes, Karen sat staring out of the hotel window across the park, reflecting on the events of the day. Then she turned out the lights and climbed between the soft sheets.

Chapter 18

Chicago
Present Time

One purpose of Karen's trip was to find an apartment, or safe house, in the Chicago area. After the operation was complete, Karen needed a place she could go that absolutely no one knew about. The first thing after breakfast, Karen looked at three apartments in the Downers Grove suburb of Chicago.

The first two were not adequate, but she rented the third under yet another of her many aliases. The apartment was ideal. It was new so the neighbors did not know each other. It was ground floor in case she had to slip out a back window. It was secluded, but still near Interstate 355, a major road that could quickly take her anywhere she wanted to go.

Karen loved art, but who could afford the originals? In today's world, good reproductions look as good as originals. They do not appreciate like the originals, but they give practically all the joy of originals, and you don't have to insure them. Karen arranged for seven great reproductions to be delivered to her new apartment.

In addition to the paintings, Karen had the manager order a living room and bedroom set from the local furniture rental company. She began planning to set up the apartment just the way she wanted. She was all by herself and did not have to consider husbands, dogs, cats, or even houseplants.

She got on her cell phone and called the various local utilities to have electricity, telephone, and internet service installed. While on the phone, the sound of someone shouting disturbed her. A few minutes later, her next door neighbor frantically knocked on the door with an emergency problem. The water was overflowing from the toilet and this girl didn't have a clue how to stop it. Karen immediately went over and turned the toilet tank valve to the off position. The neighbor didn't realize how easy it was to stop the water flow. Still, she was immensely grateful that Karen saved the day.

Karen helped her because she didn't want to make an enemy. Even though the walls were thick and sound would probably not get through, one never knew when the neighbors might see or hear something that could be compromising. Karen wanted privacy and to be left alone, but helping a neighbor helped her ability to hide. A secret agent, although making no friends, should make it her business to pleasantly converse with, and be congenial to, the people around her.

Karen greased the manager's palm with a couple of 'C-notes' and made arrangements with him to accept the various items to be delivered. Karen was happy that she now had a secure place to hide after the operation.

She drove from the Downers Grove suburb to downtown Chicago to meet with Saleh, the spokesperson for the secret group that ran the operation. They arrived separately at the Chicago Art Institute. The two huge concrete lions still guarded the Michigan Avenue entrance. They entered separately and walked through various exhibits to the back of the building to the outdoor restaurant. Now that the operation had started, this was just one of the standard precautions they took. It would be easy to spot any tag team following them through the numerous painting galleries.

Karen looked behind her as she moved through the different galleries. She looked for eyes that focused on her. This is how one knew if someone was following. When a stranger's eyes look at you, there is a problem. It is difficult, even for professionals, to keep from looking at the people they tail.

In this situation, professional tails would quickly realize the poor odds of surveillance without being exposed and give up the tail rather than blow their covers. They would then cover the exits to resume the tail when the target exited the building.

At the restaurant, they met and choose a table in the corner, near the kitchen and far away from the entrance and other tables. Out of habit, they both sat with their backs to the wall so that they could observe anyone approaching them. Saleh ordered tea with milk, in the British manner. Karen just got an iced tea. This would not be a lunch, but only a business meeting. She took a small sip and let the straw fall from her lips.

They spoke softly and went over the operational plans again, detail by detail. Nothing was in writing so it was important to be sure everyone knew their parts. Saleh wanted Karen to be intimately involved with the whole operation. He wanted her there, with the team, up until the last possible moment that she could safely get away.

"We have decided to give you a substantial bonus if everything works out correctly."

"What kind of money are we talking about?" asked Karen.

"It will be a bonus of five times our agreed salary for you."

"Did you say five times?" a stunned Karen asked.

"Yes. If everything works out we can afford to be generous."

"Damn! I'll personally see that it works."

The waitress approached the table with a basket of crusty bread in her hands and asked if they were ready to order lunch. "No," said Saleh. "We are going to leave but we will leave a generous tip." Saleh gave the waitress a twenty-dollar bill.

They rose to leave, and Saleh resisted the temptation to hug her and just shook her hand. They called taxicabs and exited separately by the lakeside rear handicapped entrance.

Chapter 19

New York
Present Time

Craig had to make the toughest decision of his life. His decision was not like which college to go to, or whether he should join the Air Force or the Navy. The decision didn't even compare to which girl to marry. For Craig, this was a decision about life and death–his life and death! There could never be a harder decision. Craig agonized over the question, but couldn't even ask others for their opinions. He promised not to tell anyone, and he was determined to keep this promise.

Craig knew that he was dying. He knew that death was the unavoidable path of every human life. But that didn't make the decision any easier.

Another problem was that the course of his disease had its ups and downs. His death would be slow. Sometimes he felt cured, and sometimes he felt terrible. But over the last couple months, the ups were lower and the downs were steeper. Today he felt well, but he knew that soon he would feel worse. He found it tough to be an optimist in his situation. How could he look at the brighter side when every day the whole world was getting darker? Could the job that Dr. Jackson offered be the solution?

He could not understand the Muslim desire to abolish all religions and political systems except their own. He was born a Roman Catholic, but had not gone to church for many years. Still, he wanted his children to be able to practice Catholicism, if they choose. One argument in favor of accepting this assignment was his desire to defend his children's right to worship God in their own way.

Craig had never given much thought to the greater questions of life and death. But now the age old questions of what is life and why was he alive invaded his mind. It wasn't really that Craig loved life that much. It was more the fear of the unknown of death.

The guilt he felt about his failure as a husband and father tipped the scale. It reduced his once high self-esteem, and now he felt inadequate. This was an opportunity to do one last thing for his family.

Just when he thought he decided, his mind flip-flopped again. A war raged in his head, the forces of life on one side, and the fear of pain and suffering on the other. It was his instinctive fear of death that made him vacillate. Time was running out, and he needed to have an answer by tomorrow.

Then there was the money. Craig had no stock portfolio to leave his wife. The house had a second mortgage and his life insurance was not enough to pay it off. Craig knew the family's dire financial situation was entirely his fault. He made good money flying planes, but he couldn't hang on to that money. It seemed to slip through his fingers. He couldn't even pay off his medical bills and his Visa card every month. If Craig didn't take Dr. Jackson's job offer, his family would really suffer, and it would be all Craig's fault.

Craig needed a good night's sleep to clear his mind and make a definite decision tomorrow. But with everything weighing him down, he couldn't relax enough to enter that restful slumber. His mind continued to replay the thoughts and arguments of the day. Finally, he decided to take a Valium, and it eventually suppressed his anguish and loosened his mind enough to allow him to drift off into a much needed sleep.

Chapter 20

Chicago
Present Time

Driving back to the airport, Karen's blue cell phone rang. "Dr. Jackson, any news?"

"He said he thought he might be able to do it! But he is not one hundred percent committed yet. There is still a part of him that just wants to crawl in a hole and die. But I think it is at least a ninety-five percent go with him."

"You just made my day," said Karen excitedly.

"He does want to meet you however," the doctor responded.

"What did you tell him about me?"

"Oh, just what we agreed on," Jackson assured her.

"OK. We need to move on this as soon as possible. Set up a meeting for Wednesday in your office after work."

Karen's mind spun. Things were working out far better and more quickly than she had imagined. There were still a ton of unresolved details, but she had to strike while the iron was hot. The plan depended on having the right people. That was more important than anything. If plan A failed, there's always plan B or plan C.

At the airport, Karen put some change in a pay phone to call Saleh on his cell. As the spokesperson for the group that hired Karen, he was her contact to advance the money needed for the venture. "We'll need the funds within one week," Karen said. "Will there be a problem getting it that fast?"

"Wonderful! Just absolutely wonderful! I will get to work on the initial funds immediately. Do you have the date of the mission set yet?"

"No, but it's looking like a go in much less than a month," Karen answered.

"We are ready to provide identification and authentic visas as soon as we get a date," Saleh assured Karen.

"I'll let you know when. How do you get authentic visas?"

"Well, one of the people I work for is a high ranking government official. He will provide them. That is all I can say," Saleh remarked.

"Sounds great! I will be in touch."

As Karen walked through security for her flight back to New York, she could hardly keep from laughing at the way airline passengers are screened. A very attractive woman in Chicago's O'Hare airport security line a few people in front of her was having a bad day. The security attendant determined that this woman needed to submit to a pat down supposedly looking for sticks of explosives taped to her body.

There must be thousands of ways to get explosives on board an airplane, and only the most non-inventive Muslim terrorist would just carry the explosives under their clothes. Taking away that poor woman's dignity was not going to make the plane safer. This woman didn't even look like a Muslim.

Back when Karen worked for the government, she saw a report of cocaine smuggled in a fake, but realistic looking, covering over a woman's abdomen. This gave the impression that she was quite pregnant instead of just carrying a load of valuable drugs. The only way she was discovered was through a tip. It could just as easily have been explosives as cocaine, and even a pat down search would not necessarily discover it.

Then there was always the possibility of an inside job. Many thousands of workers and cargo trucks bypass the rigorous screening and get in through the back entrance. Weapons can be thrown over the back fence and then retrieved by an airport worker. It would be easy for a Muslim employee to hide a weapon or explosives on board.

It is not possible to make airplanes safe. The defensive procedures that the airport screeners use against the previous type of attack are usually ineffective against the next and different attack. Being on the defensive, as airport security is, cannot always work.

Chapter 21

New York City
Present Time

Karen was very good at reading faces and watching body language. She now studied Craig intently. Karen stared into Craig's eyes, wondering what made him tick, and if he would keep his commitments. His face appeared worried and tired. It is a face deeply etched by suffering, yet there was still a look of determination and resolve.

"I am sorry to hear about your illness," Karen began. She tried to convey sympathy with her eyes. "I want to thank you for considering joining the cause of freedom. The terrorists have declared war on us, and we must defend ourselves. We must make sacrifices for our children and their children."

"Thank you. It wasn't my idea, and I don't know for sure if I can do it, but it seems I was chosen by fate," Craig's throat went dry as he replied.

There was an awkward silence as Dr. Jackson and Craig starred at Karen who finally said, "When I first heard about 9-11, I didn't think I could make a difference. The world is a lot bigger than me, and I didn't think I could change it much. Even the president, with all his power, has been unable to stop terrorism. But if this terror sickness in our world could be cured, it would have to be by someone like us who will try the impossible. That someone would not be constrained by the niceties of government. One person, in the right place at the right time, can change the course of history."

"As a pilot, I was more distressed about 9-11 than most," observed Craig. He closed his eyes and pressed on his forehead with the palm of his hand, as if he was trying to relieve a headache.

Karen continued. "We tend to think that Muslim fundamentalists killing people is something new but it's not. Since its beginning, the Muslim religion has engaged in a long series of war and intimidation against 'non-believers.' What may seem like the American war against terror, or the never-ending Pakistan-India wars, or the Israel-Palestine wars all have a common denominator of the terrorist against the infidel."

"The belief of Muslim terrorists is that Muslims must sacrifice their lives until Islam rules the world. Islamic world conquest makes all other forms of imperialism pale by comparison. Muslim fundamentalists are required to wage war against infidels. The life of an infidel is of no consequence to them. They may have temporary truces but they never abandon their war. They believe that whoever fights on the side of Islam, whether he is killed or triumphs, will have a handsome reward in heaven. How can you reason with such deluded thinking? You can't. Our only choice is something they understand, and that is from the old book, an eye for an eye."

"I heard the president or someone say that we should try to win the hearts and minds of the Muslims," offered Craig.

Karen shot Craig a look of exasperation as if she were talking to a small child. "There is a basic flaw in the concept that we should try to win the hearts and minds of Muslim fundamentals. Muslim terror has nothing to do with winning hearts and minds. This would be like trying to win the hearts and minds of Nazis in 1941. They clearly believed they were superior to us, just as Muslim fundamentals now feel superior. The only thing we can do to stop terror is to win their fear and respect, not their hearts."

"So Craig, what did you decide? Can you do this job for us?"

There was another silence that lasted about twenty seconds before Craig said, "Assuming for a minute that I will, what assurances do I have that my family will get the two million dollars? How do you plan to set it up?"

"We'll draw up a formal contract that we all sign. It will essentially look like an insurance policy payable to your wife. People get paid on large insurance policies every day, so it will not arouse any suspicion."

"It will be a policy that only pays off in the case of deaths, except not from normal human disease. Also there will be no income tax on the payoff, so the full amount will go to your wife and family. The policy can be placed in a safety deposit box in your name and you can staple a note to your will that would give instructions about the box. Additionally we will give you $100,000 cash up front money. Also, you trust Dr. Jackson and he will give his word that the money will be paid."

"Say I do," he said. "Say I fly the plane and sacrifice my life, I still need to know the details of the mission."

"It's a simple plan. Simplicity is our friend and complexity the enemy for any plan. We will only have three people and no traditional weapons to smuggle or conccal. We have high connections that will assist in our success. Another advantage is the results of the plan. There are a number of possible results and each could be called a success. The plan is exquisite."

"What will the plan do?"

"It's just a repayment to the terrorists. They think they beat the Soviets in Afghanistan and the Soviet Union was overthrown. They think they beat America and England in Iraq and caused change of governments. They think that terror cannot be answered, and this emboldens them to commit further atrocities and beheadings. They think that they are safe because they are not a country that can be attacked. They will discover that it's their own blood they smell, and they will not go to heaven with 72 virgins, but go straight to hell. They believe that we are defenseless, but we will prove them wrong. We will crash a plane into one of their buildings. Like I said, an eye for an eye. It will make them think twice before unleashing terror on America again.

"It will really upset the Muslim fundamentalists and make them rethink their strategy of world domination. Hopefully they'll see real problems in their use of terror. The whole point is to give the moderates some ammunition to use against the more fundamental leaders."

"You don't have many months of life left. No known treatment will work to save you. Spare yourself unnecessary pain and suffering. Accept your destiny."

"I don't know what to say. But, OK, I will pilot the plane. Today I think I can do it but tomorrow? I'm not sure how I will feel tomorrow. But OK, let's do it." There was both sadness and resolve in Craig's voice.

"Great," said Karen. "It's the only decision you could reasonably make. I'm going to take a few photos of you so that we can set up an alias identification. I have the contacts to get passports, driver's licenses, work visas, and everything we will need."

Karen left the conference that afternoon in an exalted mood. She had a feeling of accomplishment in the new developments, a sense that it was all coming together.

Chapter 22

New York City
Present Time

The red phone rings and Sevorov sounds pleased. "We got the money. When do you think we will be flying?"

"My sources will get their schedule any time now. It will probably be in a week or less." Sevorov was under the impression that Nick and he would hijack an airplane that had some high level terrorists on it. Then the plane would be flown to a friendly airstrip. Sevorov and Nick would be the muscle, and they believed Karen's pilot would help deliver the plane to friendly forces. Then they would go back to Russia, rich men.

"Did you try out the make-up?" Sevorov was a huge powerful looking man. In order to look less intimidating when boarding the plane, he would dye his hair white and darken his completion with a few applications of self-tanning lotion. He would also practice a stooped old man look by hunching over and walking with a cane and a limp.

"Looks authentic."

"Then take some pictures for the IDs. E-mail the pictures to me and we will be all set."

Karen was excited. This was, by far, the biggest and most important operation of her entire career. Everything was on track and the quick progress exceeded her most optimistic expectations. Next on Karen's agenda was the MP3 audio file that would take credit and give reasons for the attack. The first step here is to create a storyboard or outline of the audio. Karen would do the speaking, but of course her voice would be completely altered.

After she was satisfied with the audio file she would put it through a software program called Vocal Imitation. This is a software module that allows the user to imitate vocal characters segments from one person into other person voice in such a way that a second person's voice will be heard speaking in the same voice as the first person. This powerful tool is based on robust algorithms that provides flexible vocal files and brings new concept to the dubbing post production sound effects.

She decided to keep the voice a woman's since the concept of a female in charge of terrorists would be all the more insulting to the macho Muslim culture. The audio file would be edited in three different ways. Each would take credit for a different result of the operation. The actual results would appear to be the plan all along. The various files would be completed prior to the mission so that it could immediately be sent to various news organizations. 'Lots to do and so little time,' thought Karen.

Airline tickets to Athens, Greece, hotel reservations in Athens, tickets, and work visas to Saudi Arabia - so many details, but Karen got it done. That's her specialty. She knows how to get things done.

Now that the dates were confirmed, Karen phoned Saleh to tell him the good news. "We're all set to go. I hoped that we can do it on September eleventh, but we cannot wait. We will be in Athens in three days, and the operation will begin the next day. I will keep you informed of any changes."

"We wish you God's speed," said Saleh. "Remember to go to a public internet computer, like in an internet café, coffee house, library, or hotel and preferably not your own hotel. Outgoing messages should be written on a word processor, then coded, and then copied and pasted into an e-mail file to avoid keeping the computer online for a long time. Incoming messages should likewise be copied from e-mail and pasted to a word processor and decoded. Let us know if anything doesn't work out. It is vital we know as soon a possible so we can make adjustments."

"Worry not. I'm checking out everything. But if the unexpected occurs, I will contact you immediately."

Chapter 23

New York Suburb (Maplewood)
Present Time

Maplewood, New Jersey is a quiet picturesque, little suburb that maintains something of a country-home aesthetic. Like the town, the pedestrian-friendly downtown district is small, but filled with quaint stores. Maplewood is about a 35 minute train trip to New York, but its real estate is much more affordable.

Craig and his family live in a charming brick Colonial style house with white trim, and light green shutters. The streets are lined with charming big shade trees, outstanding shrubbery, and well-kept homes. The soft sound of metal wind chimes in the gentle breeze brings a peaceful ambiance to the house. Brilliant red roses and neatly trimmed bushes add dignity to the front garden.

Craig walked purposefully up the flagstone walkway, past the neatly tended beds of colorful flowers, and opened his front door and stepped into the spotlessly clean home.

Inside, he stopped in the foyer to remove his coat. As usual, Snowball was the first to hear him. Snowball is a thirteen-pound Bichon Frise who thinks she is a person. She growled and barked a few seconds, then realized who it was. She wagged her tail as she made a beeline for Craig. He stooped down and Snowball bounded into his arms. Craig hugged her knowing that Snowball could always be counted on for unconditional love. She was not a serious watchdog but only a gentle, loving lap dog who doesn't have a mean bone in her body.

As Craig hugged Snowball, he asked himself how many birthdays and Christmas seasons he missed while piloting an airplane here and there? He always said he worked such long hours for the family, but he knew he could have been home more. Time passed them by and they never spent enough of it together. Somehow other pilots managed to spend more time with their families.

His wife Joan is in her late thirties and about ten years younger than Craig. She has an uncommon strength that allows her to overlook Craig's little boy ways. She is a kind and gentle woman, full of compassion for Craig, even when she coped with his dalliances with another woman that she once found out about. He said he was sorry and would never do it again and she forgave him. Since his illness, Craig wondered why those sexual encounters ever had power over him. Maybe it was the medication or the worry about his impending death, but now erotic images and thoughts quickly dissipate and have no power over him.

Joan has a youthful quality of innocence in her knowing eyes that makes her seem younger than she is. Even after years of marriage, Craig still thinks that she is quite cute in her khaki shorts and white shirt. Unfortunately, their marriage had never been blessed with intense passion. Craig always felt cheated that somehow he was missing this important part of a marriage. But now his passions for her are gone. He still hopes he can rekindle his passions tonight but deep in his heart he knows they will never return.

"How are you feeling?" Joan asked, with a warm smile, as she entered the living room. She knew that Craig had recently complained about the steady decline of his stamina and strength.

It is a strange time; it is a totally bizarre time, but he knew that his destiny was inescapable. He knew he couldn't tell Joan the truth. "I still don't believe this is really happening to me, but I'm doing better today," Craig said quietly.

Kerwood, their four old daughter, ran into the living room and raised her hands indicating the desire to be picked up and greeted. Craig picked her up for a hug and delighted in her youthful exuberance. It's easier to pick Kerwood up than put her down, but after the third try she let go and Craig put her down.

A few minutes later Craig's eight-year-old son ran into the room. His son's name is Landry, and Craig thought it strange that both his children had unusual and genderless first names, but Joan insisted because she wanted them to be unique. Craig thought it would hinder the kids but, as usual, gave Joan her way.

Craig gave Joan a hug and a light peck on the mouth. Then he kicked off his black SAS shoes and walked over to his favorite chair. He sank back in the deeply padded seat, and as usual, Joan sat on the couch. Craig had to keep his hands on the arm rest because each time that he lowered his hands, Snowball licked his fingers, partly in affection, but also because she wanted to be picked up again.

Craig looked at Joan and said, "Your eyes, they look so red. Have you been crying?"

"No," she lied. "My allergies kick in this time of the year and cause my eyes to look red."

Craig accepted this answer because he didn't want to think of the alternative. "I am going out of town for about a week. I have an appointment with a new doctor who specializes in my particular illness," Craig said "There might still be a way out of this death sentence."

Craig had no intention of telling Joan about the real trip he would take. She will learn about it soon enough. He knew that Joan would try to talk him out of it, so better not to even bring it up. He will shield her from the true hopelessness of the situation.

Joan noticed that Craig recently developed sadness in his eyes and a defeatist slump in his shoulders. "You have to keep a positive mind," she said as her eyes glistened.

"What do I have to be positive about?" asked Craig.

"Craig!" replied Joan in a strong voice. It was a request for Craig to understand that he can have a positive attitude regardless of the circumstances he is in.

"Be an optimist. Last week I read a quote about the definitive optimist. It took place long ago in Bourbon, France. There was a man sentenced to death by the king, but the man knew that the king had a horse that he really loved so the man said to the king, "I know the secrets of animals and I can make your horse talk. It will take six months but I will do it if you spare my life." Well, the King liked the idea and told the man that he would stay the execution."

"Later, the man's friends asked him why he told the king such a stupid thing. The man said, "Instead of dying tomorrow I will be alive for six months. Six months is a long time. In six months, the king may die and the new ruler will let me live. In six months, I may die of natural causes. Or in six months the horse might talk.

"You just have to look at the possibilities and never give up."

Craig noded in agreement and smiled, but he knew that his decision was already made. The man in the story wasn't going to have six months of excruciating pain. Craig knew he would have no quality of life and just wanted to get it over with.

Today they were closer together than they had been for some years. The wood fireplace crackled and its romantic flickering light played on the ceiling. But there were secrets they keep from each other, and therefore, they did not have true communication.

For the last few months Craig had been having difficulties. It might be the medication he took or it could be his nervous state of mind. He never had these difficulties prior to his illness, but now it was a problem, so in preparation for the evening he swallowed a Viagra.

Later that evening Craig made an effort, but the Viagra didn't seem to work. It was really embarrassing, but Joan said it was all right. Craig knew that it wasn't.

Behind her frozen smile, he knew she felt a great hurt. He would have given almost anything to be able to take her in his arms and really talk and coax the hurt out of her. But he could not. He could not take the emotions. He could never handle these strong emotions.

Craig had previously written a letter and given it to one of his best friends to deliver to Joan in the event of his death. That letter would tell of his love and also of the money she would receive. It would give details of the deposits in her name at the Maerki Baumann & Co. Bank located in Zurich, Switzerland. But now he could not stand the emotions that would come with an honest communication.

He looked back over the years of his marriage and knew he was not a good husband. As an airline pilot he spent many days in far off hotels. Craig was not overly handsome in a classical sense, but the local women seemed to be pulled to his uniform with the gold buttons. Some flight attendants also chased Craig, and often caught him. Maybe his terminal illness was God's punishment for his gambling and adultery over the years. Maybe his final sacrifice would turn the tally back in his favor.

When Craig got up from bed, he immediately turned his back to Joan so she could not see the look of sadness on his face. There were tears in his eyes and they started to run down his cheeks. He quickly walked down the hall to the bathroom, got a Kleenex, and blew his nose.

Chapter 24

New York City
Present Time

At JFK airport Karen checked a suitcase containing both body armor shirts. She waited in line with her wooden cane and cell phone. The battery compartment of the cell phone had three thin razor blades positioned together so they just looked like one piece of metal. Even an x-ray would see only a metal case and not the three blades. "Put your keys and other metal objects in the plastic container," said a bored looking woman who probably made close to minimum wage. "Take your shoes off. Put your computer in the basket."

Karen quickly complied, and even put her wooden cane on the conveyer belt, and limped through the metal detector. The irony of requiring that she take off her shoes, while letting her bring a very strong wooden cane onboard without even one question about the cane was not lost on Karen.

All cell phones already have some metal in them so they are treated like keys and pocket change. They are put in the plastic container, skip the metal detector, and instead go through the x-ray machine.

Karen wore a navy blue blazer and open-collared white blouse. She thought that this was a conservative business suit that was designed to make her invisible. She did not want to look like someone who would require close examination by airport security. Everything went like clockwork, and Karen put her cell phone back in her pocket and retrieved her carry on luggage, cane, and computer.

Flight 132 left New York at 5:45 PM, only fifteen minutes late, which was good for that time of the day. It would take almost ten hours for the non-stop to reach Athens. Karen felt good that she was going on a secret mission "in-country."

The flight attendant made her rounds soliciting beverages and Karen asked for a Coke. A baby across the aisle started screaming. Its mother tried to comfort him by rocking him in her arms, but to no avail. Eventually he went to sleep.

The Boeing 767-300 was comfortable and the dinner good, considering it was airline food. The man sitting next to Karen tried to start a conversation, but people in Karen's profession do not engage in idle talk with strangers. Karen grunted a bit and went back to looking at her *Forbes* magazine. Later she would go to sleep. One foolproof way to avoid conversation with people sitting around you is to sleep on the airplane.

The magazine was only a prop and Karen wasn't engrossed in it. She daydreamed about herself and her life. Karen speculated on how this operation would affect her future. It would be a brilliant operation, but no one could ever find out that she did it. This bothered Karen because recognition was a powerful motivator for her. She loved the awards she won working for the government, but in this job there would be no recognition. There would just be money. Still, there would be a lot of money, but she already knew she did not want to retire. Something would have to turn up. Possibly Saleh would have another job for her.

For most of her life Karen couldn't sleep on airplanes. The best cure for jet lag is to sleep on the plane and wake up in the morning in Europe. But wanting to sleep is different from sleeping. She really had to learn to sleep in a chair and in public. It took many airplane trips but she finally got the hang of it.

After dinner Karen put on her black eye cover, noise-canceling earphones, and listened to a very long meditative piece of music from her iPhone. She slept deeply.

Chapter 25

Athens Greece
Present Time

Most frequent long distance flyers know that traveling east across the Atlantic Ocean is harder than going west. The jet lag syndrome adjusts better to a long day than a short one. Even during the best of times, sleep deprivation could irritate people and cause them to perform poorly. As an ex-pilot whose job it was to stay awake, Craig never learned to sleep as well as Karen. Craig couldn't sleep a wink.

Craig's Boeing 747 touched down at an airport just outside Athens three hours late, due to a late start and headwinds over the Atlantic Ocean. Craig was a professional and knew about delays, but today, with the jet lag, and with the deadly seriousness of his mission, it really upset him. He just wanted to get this thing over with, but so far there was delay, and more delay.

Sometimes life moves too slowly and sometimes life is too short. Sometimes the world gives you much too much to cope with. This was one of those times. "Why don't things just work out? Why am I dying? What is the answer to life and death?" These questions, but no answers, enveloped Craig's consciousness.

Karen, Craig, Sevorov, and Nick would all spend the night in Athens. Sevorov and Nick stayed at the same hotel. Everyone else stayed at different hotels, but Karen would visit them all.

Tomorrow morning, they would see each other for a few moments at the airport. Just long enough so the Russians would know what Craig looked like, but not long enough for any camera or anyone possibly following the Russians to put anything together.

Karen chose really nice quaint, picturesque hotels, but not the five stars variety. Those are far too glitzy and public, often with paparazzi checking for celebrities. One level below the five star hotels offered great accommodations, great treatment, and most importantly, privacy.

Karen phoned Sevorov at their hotel and was happy that they made it to Athens with no problems. "Are you ready for me to come visit you?"

"No problem. When will you be here?"

"About an hour."

"Our room number is 520. Come on up."

Karen always thought that Athens looked poor compared to most major European cities. She remembered on her last visit, the center lanes of a major street were piled high with litter and rubble, but today, riding in the taxi to visit Sevorov, she was impressed with the changes made in Athens as a result of the 2004 Summer Olympics.

Arriving at the hotel, Karen gave the standard tip to the taxi driver. To remain unnoticed, you blend in with those around you. The tip should not be too big or too small. 'Fit in and don't be an outside' is the rule when in country doing a job.

Karen knocked on the door and waited a short time. Sevorov finished drinking his beer and easily crushed the can in his strong hand before throwing it towards the garbage can, but his shot missed. He opened the door and flashed his big trademark grin, showing his bright white teeth.

"Hello, Karen!"

"Sevorov, it's good to finally meet you," Karen said, giving a grin back. Sevorov was a powerfully built grizzly bear of man. He extended his huge hand and it enveloped Karen's, giving her a strong hearty handshake. Karen heard that Sevorov continued to feel bad about the difficult time he had in the Chechnya fighting and his expulsion from the army. The experience carved in his face and his eyes seemed hard, cold, and unforgiving.

His expression changed and his voice had a touch of anger when he spoke, "I will be glad when I can get rid of this gray color and go back to my natural good-looking black. And as far as that dark sunless tanning lotion is concerned, I never want to look like an Arab again."

Then suddenly Sevorov's expression changed back and he flashed his trademark smile. "Let me introduce you to Nick."

Karen was somewhat surprised at Nick's small size. She knew he wouldn't be as big as Sevorov, but Nick looked to be about five foot seven and appeared to weigh no more than one hundred and forty pounds. Dressed in slacks and a white turtleneck and clean-shaven with fine skin, he looked more like the kid next door. Sevorov saw the worry in Karen's face and said, "He looks small but he is solidly built and also an expert at his profession."

Nick walked over slowly to shake hands with Karen, and his movements had an athlete's easy grace. His handshake was firm and manly. With the handshake was an easy smile that relaxed Karen. Also, there was something else about him. His eyes were the coolest, clearest blue eyes that Karen ever saw. In those eyes was definite fearlessness and intelligence.

Karen smiled back and observed Nicks focused intensity. She knew that some of the best fighters were small, but highly trained. Still, big and highly trained is even better for this mission. Alas, there was nothing Karen could do now, so she just trusted that, in spite of his small size, Nick was as good as promised.

Karen took a package out of her briefcase. "Let me show you this great body armor. There is a company named Miguel Caballero LTD and it is located in Bogotá, Columbia. They make what's called high security fashion. As you know, Columbia has a lot of violence, and therefore, a need for body armor. They make ordinary business and casual attire clothes out of body armor material. What I have here looks like regular white T-shirts. One is large and one XXX large. They are model 40600 and they will stop a 9 mm Uzi submachine gun that sends out slugs at speeds of 1250 feet per second. They will easily stop anything a air marshal has on board."

"Looks damn good. I can't believe they're so light."

"Yes, only a few pounds. Try them on and see how they fit."

Karen was concerned that even the triple extra large would not fit Sevorov, but he easily got into it. Nick's was a bit too large, but not so big as to call attention to the clothes. They would wear their normal shirts over the T-shirt, so no one would suspect anything.

"I wore the large-sized one on the plane from New York, and they go through the metal detector with no problem. Let me show you the cane."

Karen handed the cane to Sevorov who examined it and nodded his head in approval. It was solid and weighed a lot for a wood cane. The handle was the same wood bent in a crook so there was no metal in it. A long brown rubber cap covered the tip of the cane. Karen removed the cap from the cane to show Sevorov the three groves cut in the wood.

"Now look closely at this cell phone. Watch while I remove the battery compartment. Now notice the small steel plate between the phone and the battery. You take out the steel plate, and it easily snaps apart into three very sharp blades. But here's the really neat part. Each of the plates snaps in one of the precut wood slots on the cane. They stay in very well all by themselves, but on the airplane put some of this quick setting epoxy glue in the groves before you snap in the blades. They will stay even better with the glue. We experimented with this, and the glue makes it really strong. Here are two small plastic containers that you mix together to form the epoxy. It is a fast acting epoxy that sets up in only a few minutes. Just put them in your carry on and take them out once you have gone through security."

"Looks like a great weapon. I'm impressed. It's a combination of a deadly, razor sharp, short spear and a cane. In my hands, this is capable of doing a lot of damage."

"I'll take it apart, and you try putting it together a few times. You'll put it together in the rest room, and then put this brown plastic bag over the tip, so no one notices. At the last minute you just take the bag off, and you have your perfect weapon."

Sevorov had no trouble putting it together, so Karen put the blades back in the cell phone and handed the cane to Sevorov. "Let's see you walk like an old man."

Sevorov grinned and did a very good imitation of someone who needed a cane to walk any distance. "Now let's review the plan. The entire plan was designed to minimize the possibility of anything going wrong. Whenever possible we will use the KISS principle. It's just an acronym for 'keep it simple, stupid.' The perception we want to present to everyone is that you are not a dangerous person, but instead old and weak. Even the deadly weapon, the cane, makes it appear that you are weak."

"Remember we expect six terrorist money men to board. I will be at the airport, and if the terrorists do not board, I will tell you and the operation will abort. We will still pay you half your agreed fee just for showing up. If I do not say anything to you, they are in the airport and the operation will go forward."

Karen showed Sevorov and Nick over fifty pictures. There were over two dozen pictures of the interior of the McDonnell Douglas MD-90. Pictures of the cockpit, bathroom, and first class section, there were pictures of everything. There were even pictures of the security screening station and the waiting room. Nothing was left to chance.

"The terrorists do not know that we have identified them so, chances are, they will not resist. However if they do, our planning will still have the advantage. They will be completely unarmed. We won't."

Karen led them through the entire plan of attack and reviewed the alternative plans and the timing in minute detail. Then she said,

"When you get to the airport waiting room, look for Craig. He will wear a blue American style baseball cap, and just nod to him. He only speaks English so don't try to speak to him. Besides, airports have many cameras and we don't want anyone to think that a number of people who know each other are getting on board.

"Remember, once we get control of the plane, Craig will fly very low to prevent radar detection. Flying is his job, so let him do the flying, and your job is to control the passengers. Craig is not very strong, and he is not a fighter, so don't count on him helping you with the passengers.

"We have a deserted airstrip just over the border in Iraq. Once the plane lands in Iraq we have everything taken care of. We have some armed agents and drivers with trucks that will take the six or so prisoners from you. They will have pictures of the terrorists we expect on board, so they can identify them. There will also be a truck and driver to take you to Kuwait where we have arranged a hotel and tickets to England, and then back to Russia. The remaining passengers will be freed. Any questions?"

"How about new passports to get back to Russia?"

"In Kuwait we will have passports, tickets, and all the documentation that you will need waiting for you. Anything else?"

"No," Sevorov muttered, and after a moment said, "We are going downstairs for a drink and dinner. We might even find some Ambur Starka Vodka. Do you want to come?"

Karen knew what these soldiers meant by a drink. The ordinary Russian soldier drank enough to meet the normal criteria of an alcoholic. Sevorov probably meant ten drinks and dinner. Drinking together is important for soldiers. Getting a little drunk helps build a strong bond and that is the key for people who will put their lives on the line for each other. Without that bond, very few people would risk their lives.

"I can't make it because I'm going over to review the plans with Craig, but have a good time, and get a good night's sleep. My number is 210 9264397. Phone me if you think of any questions or have any problems. Otherwise I will see you at the airport tomorrow."

The rest of the truth is that Karen did not want to be seen in public with Sevorov. If Sevorov were identified by an airport camera, any public communication with him would put Karen at risk. Additionally, Karen had a problem internalizing the concept of sending people, unknowingly, to their death. Call it a personality flaw or a mark of civilization; Karen had to leave as soon as she possibly could.

Five minutes later, Karen was in front of the hotel, hailing a cab, and the Russians were in the hotel bar ordering their first round of vodka. They traded stories of their experiences in the Russian army and ordered round after round of refills. Others at the bar noticed them, but no one else spoke Russian and their conversations were not about their assignment tomorrow.

After a short taxi ride, Karen was back at her hotel. Upon arriving, she sent a message from the free internet computer room off the main lobby. It was addressed to one of Karen's clean Yahoo accounts. "Uncle Santa, this is Clause. The sun is rising, and we're doing well. Tomorrow is a go, and it looks good. I will contact you immediately if there is a problem."

Chapter 26

Athens, Greece
Present Time

Karen took a cab to Craig's hotel for their last confidence building session. Karen put him up at the Athenaeum Inter-Continental Hotel. It is centrally located, near the other hotels, and only 22 kilometers from the airport.

She was surprised to find Craig smoking a cigarette. "I figured that this stuff won't hurt me anymore," Craig said as he saw Karen's puzzled look. Karen thought that this was a good sign since Craig appeared to accept that tomorrow would be his last day. He had come here to die. Still dying is final, and there is always the possibility that Craig would panic and change his mind. Karen decided that she needed to keep a close eye on Craig.

Craig was the only one who knew he would die tomorrow so he was the key. Karen looked deeply into Craig's face as he spoke. "Remember Craig, don't talk to the Russians. Their entire job is just to secure the airplane and retain control of it. They do not know this is a one way mission."

"Well, what if they find out?"

"They won't find out. I told them that you would be flying low to escape radar detection. They don't speak any English, so don't try to communicate in any way. Once you are in the cockpit, if the door is not broken, lock it."

"Ok, ok, I can do it."

"Good. Let's review the plan. Your target is only ten or so minutes from the plane's normal destination of Jeddah, Saudi Arabia. I have written down the coordinates of your target which are 21°25.64 north latitude and 39°48.89 east longitude. You will be able to use your GPS system to steer the plane towards the target.

"When you get close you can manually take over. This city is located in a narrow valley and is surrounded by hills from 200 to 500 ft. high. Your target is about fifty feet in height. Here is an aerial map of the city and the target within it. The topography will help guide you during the last minute or so of your flight.

"Tie your shoes extra tight. We don't want you tripping tomorrow. Take all metal objects out of your pockets, so that you are not stopped at the screening area."

Most sane people like money, and will do a lot for the security and comfort that money brings. Still, there is a moral line that the sane person will not cross even for lots of money. The best enticement is a combination of money and moral certitude. Combine that with the guilt Craig felt for his abandonment of his family, and you have the conditions for action. Karen understood personalities and motivation and knew this about Craig. Consequently, she thought it prudent to give a last anti-Muslim terrorist pep talk.

"I want to review the reasons we're here tonight preparing to sacrifice our lives. It is to protect our children and their children so they can live in freedom.

"The Muslim belief system was founded on war and extremism and remains true to its roots. Even modern Muslims do not separate church from state and are intolerant of non-Muslims. The results are the last 1400 years of conflict and today's threat to civilized life.

"The killing of infidels began during Muhammad's life and has continued ever since. In the year 1009, there was the Muslim destruction of the Church of the Holy Sepulcher and most of the Christian churches in Jerusalem. For years thereafter Christians were cruelly persecuted. Killing, destroying, raping and plundering of Christians were the norm. The various Christian Crusades were expeditions undertaken to retake the Holy Places seized by terrorists.

"I'm afraid I have absolutely no idea what the Church of the Holy Sepulcher is. I must have missed that in Sunday school," said Craig.

"The Church of the Holy Sepulcher is the church that was built over the place where Jesus had been crucified and buried. It was considered to be one of the most holy places in Christianity," replied Karen. "The entire Middle East was stolen by murder and force from us non-Muslims, and there was never any payment for this stolen land.

"Speaking of the Middle East, in 1940 there were over one million Jews living in Muslim countries. Today there are almost none left. Over one half million of these Jews escaped to Israel.

"Islamic fanatics killed over a half million infidels in Indonesia in 1965. Over a million infidels were killed in Africa by Muslims during the last ten years, and the list could go on and on.

"Today, Muslim terrorism targeting civilians around the world threaten our very freedom. Their savage killing of civilians cannot be allowed to continue. We spend years in hunting down and killing one terrorist, and he is replaced by ten more."

"Do you really think that we can make a difference by fighting back?"

"Oh, without a doubt! There is no other choice. Let me tell you about Buddhism.

"Buddha was born and lived in India, but did you ever wonder why there are no Buddhist left there? The terrorists killed them, destroyed their temples, and built mosques over them."

"Muslims first attacked India about the year 712. They demolished Buddhists and Hindu temples and killed hundreds of thousands of people. The Muslims then built mosques on top of the demolished temples. The peaceful Buddhists have an acceptance of death that helps them find personal peace. Consequently, they did not fight back very well against the savage Muslims, so they were eventually slaughtered. The Buddhists who escaped the massacres found refuge in Tibet and Nepal. Over the following centuries many millions of Buddhists were executed in India by Muslim invaders.

"There were once even many Buddhists who lived in Afghanistan. Who can forget the pictures of Muslim terrorists destroying that giant 175 ft tall sandstone statue of Buddha carved into the cliffs at Bamiyan, Afghanistan, West of Kabul? The Muslims delighted in repeatedly hitting it with cannon fire."

"Well, what does that have to do with fighting back?"

"During the same violence, terrorists tried to kill the Hindus, but unlike the peaceful Buddhists, the Hindus fought back resulting in huge periodic massacres of one side or the other. One mountain range in eastern Afghanistan, where many thousands of Hindus were killed, is still called Hindu Kush, which translates to 'Hindu Slaughter.' So you see, if no one fights back the Muslims will just kill, destroy, win, and enslave."

"Well, yes, I have heard about the many Muslim-Hindu wars but what about us Christians? Isn't our history also savage?"

"Yes, during the dark ages some Christians were no better than the Muslims, but in the last number of centuries, Christianity has really advanced. The problem is that Islam is still in the dark ages, but now they have modern weapons. They still commit barbaric acts of beheading innocent civilians and shooting small children in the back.

The God who created mankind wouldn't deceive him or lead mankind to hell as Allah does, nor would he order men to terrorize, mutilate, and slaughter the followers of other belief systems."

"Why didn't the Muslims come into the modern age?"

"In the late 1930s, vast deposits of oil were discovered in the Middle East. At the time the Muslims were still a primitive and nomadic people, very similar to the rough and severe people who lived in the seventh century dark ages. The oil gave these primitive people money and tried to push civilization upon them. However, the oil was a curse and kept the Muslims from having to work and advance in the modern world.

"Muslim fundamentalists think that with terrorism they are now strong. They believe that terror defeated the Soviet Union and it dissolved into Russia and other states. They believe they beat America in Iraq.

"Radical Muslims have created a fiction that it is not Islam or some country committing these acts, but just some terrorists. They believe that civilized countries will not be able to fight back, because the terrorists hide and can't be found."

"Why not just steal a rocket or missile? Why do you need a passenger plane?"

"It's a physiological thing. A rocket would do some damage, but a plane is payback in full. It will destroy the fiction that Islam is strong, because only they are willing to kill and die for their beliefs. It will show that free men are also willing to kill and die.

"Our goal is to expose the truth that Islam is still weak. Countries, because they are civilized, may not be able to effectively fight back against terror, but individual groups can. And we know the terror headquarters are located in the mosques where the mullahs preach the concept of Islamic world domination. These mosques are high profile and not well defended. They are weak and they are in our sights!

"So what is the solution when fanatic Muslim fundamentalists target civilians instead of military targets and are not condemned by their fellow Muslims?

"You have to say that enough is enough. We will not tolerate this carnage anymore. The only solution is to answer the terrorist war on civilians with our own war on select targets. The only thing that kept America and the Soviets from war was the knowledge of quick and powerful retaliation. They called it MAD for mutual assured destruction.

"Only in this way will we isolate and marginalize the Muslim extremists. Only in this way will the Muslim moderates be motivated to point out the terrorists in their midst. With an eye for an eye reaction by free people, the terrorist will not be seen as a martyr but instead as a destroyer of his own family, church, and country. Then Muslims who hear of terrorism against infidels, will stop dancing in the street and run to turn in these barbaric killers."

"Yes," said Craig, "They have to be stopped."

"Remember to stay focused tomorrow. All you have to do is fly the plane, and the Russians will take care of the rest. Just focus on the plane." Karen smiled and gave Craig a comforting pat on the shoulder. "Try to get a good night's sleep. Tomorrow we will change the world," she said. "I will phone you tomorrow to be sure you wake up OK. If you need me for any reason my number is 210 9264397." Then she left Craig's room knowing that she had a motivated operative.

After Karen left, Craig dead bolted and chained the door. He turned and looked into an old streaked mirror and studied his reflection. He did not know who he was. Exhausted, he fell into the bed and curled up. Now it was up to Craig to determine if he was strong enough to do his duty for mankind. Craig thought the answer was yes, but it would be a long night.

Chapter 27

Athens, Greece
The Final Night

The sky opened up with flashes of lightning that illuminated the darkening city. Thunder, so loud you couldn't hear yourself think, periodically boomed and reverberated within the building. Craig went to bed and lay curled in a fetal position, staring at the reflections of lightning off the white walls and listened to the sound of the rain that made a rhythmic arrangement on his hotel window. Normally the thunder and the pitter-patter of rain would quickly put him to sleep, but this evening the soothing effect of the rain did not mesmerize him, and sleep would not come.

He picked up the phone and called room service for a bottle of wine. He needed the alcohol, for tomorrow he would begin the last day on earth, and as a terrorist who gave his life to protect his family.

As he drank, he thought back and the whole situation, his entire life, seemed so absurd. He always knew life was perplexing and often challenging, but this situation was far more than just perplexing. It was downright absurd and made absolutely no sense. A chill went through him as he contemplated dying all alone in a strange country. There was a pain coming from his chest. He breathed deeply, trying to control the involuntary trembling that seized his entire body.

He sat up and thought about calling Karen and saying that he just couldn't do it. He started to call her, but then muttered to himself, "To hell with it!" Still depressed, he crawled back into bed.

Craig still couldn't sleep. How could you sleep when you knew that you had less than twenty-four hours to live? How could you sleep when you knew that tomorrow's action could change the course of world history? Instead of sleep, frightening visions of tomorrow invaded his mind. The air seemed oppressive and difficult to breath. Every breath was a struggle. He pressed his fisted hands on each side of his head, to drown out the visions, but the visions remained. He remembered what his mother told him many years ago. "If you can't fall asleep, just keep your eyes shut and lay there. Quiet rest is as good as sleep." But Craig couldn't lie quietly. He squirmed and thrashed and sleep still would not descend upon him.

During the last month and a half, he did a lot of thinking about death. He studied it from many viewpoints, trying in vain to find a solution to his dilemma. This suicide mission seemed to be the only way he could beat the agony of a very painful death. The thoughts went around and around. Anxiety, insomnia and fear, it was a difficult night. He tucked himself in again and pulled his blanket up so that it touched his lower lip. This usually relaxed him, just as a bottle relaxed a baby, but tonight nothing worked. He looked at the illuminated digits on the hotel's clock. It said 4:18. Soon it would be light and he was still wide awake.

He wished he wasn't sick. He wished he was younger. He wished that his hair hadn't fallen out. But he knew wishing wouldn't help. He knew that each tick of the clock was bringing him closer to tomorrow and he hoped to God he could perform his duties. By six o'clock, the rain ended and now all that was left was the fresh scent of the rain and ozone produced by the lightning.

He hadn't slept a wink and was still obsessed with his quickly approaching death. What had been the point of life if it was going to end like this? Craig was never a religious man. In fact, he hated the times when his mother forced him to attend Sunday church services. Still, death was the great mystery and Craig had to find a way to deal with it. Everyone would die, but for most people the event was so far away that they did not dwell on it. But for Craig, death was today.

He was irritated with himself. He knew he hadn't been a good husband or father. What in his life caused him to wander with other women? What came over him? He shook his head and drew a long breath. He hoped the ultimate sacrifice he planned to make would balance the books. Or would this just be another escape from the pain and suffering that would surely devastate him as he died of cancer? So many questions and there were no answers. That was the story of his life, questions without answers.

As gloom descended, he thought that he could still change his mind. But deep within, he knew that this was the best thing he could do for his family. It's not like his life could ever return to normal. He was dying and the pain would be terrible. Why me? he thought. My God in heaven, why me?

Finally he could lie in bed no more, and he drew open the curtains. He had a good view of the park across the square and saw that the rain had changed into a clear morning sky that flaunted its sunrise splendor of blue and gold like a banner over Athens. This would be the defining day of his life. This would be his last day of life.

Craig got up, phoned room service and then sat on his bed, using all the pillows as a backrest. He turned the television on to one of the two English-speaking stations, but he didn't really watch it. Instead he just used the television as a comforting background while he reviewed his predicament in his mind for the umpteenth time.

Because of his terminal illness, Craig's body felt feeble and weak. But in his heart he hoped he had the strength to fulfill his destiny and be the hero that he wished he was. "Be brave," he told himself. Today's action could very well alter the course of history.

Most mornings he read the paper and did a number of calisthenics and isometric exercises to keep his body strong. There didn't seem to be any point in doing any of that today. News was meaningless and his body only needed to last one day. Rehearsing the words he would use at the airport, he steeled himself for the ordeal that lay ahead. Still trying to relax, he poured cream into a cup of hot and strong coffee and drank it slowly.

Chapter 28

Athens, Greece
The Final Night

People who don't plan are doomed to failure before they start. Karen went over and over the various possibilities of tomorrow's actions in her mind. It was making her crazy. It was so quiet that she couldn't stop thinking. She grabbed the television remote and flipped quickly through the channels. She found a French news show, so she stopped her television surfing there. It was one of those talking head news shows that was really more entertainment than news. These shows pick topics that are of interest to the largest possible audience.

Karen couldn't get away from it. The discussion was about the upcoming election in England. Would the recent terrorist attack there sway the election, and if so, which way?

One of the talking heads compared England and Spain. "On March 11, 2004 terrorists set off bombs on four commuter trains in Madrid, Spain. They killed 191 innocent civilians and injured many more. Three days later, in the Spanish elections, the existing party was defeated, and a party whose leaders promised to withdraw all troops from Iraq was elected. The Islamic goal to change the government in a free country succeeded even better than their expectations."

The other talking head said, "Radical Muslims had once sent armies to Spain, conquering most of it and resulting in much death and destruction. Therefore the Spanish are more afraid of Muslims than the British. The British experience during the nineteenth and twentieth centuries was that the Muslims were poor fighters and easily defeated, by a well-disciplined army."

The third talking head added, "With the advent of the passenger jet liner, ruthless Muslims have found a weakness and are exploiting it. Airport security searches are about as transparent to a truly dedicated terrorist as a child's scheming is transparent to an parent. There are literally thousands of ways to bring weapons on board. Even the current definition of a weapon is deficient to anyone able to scheme and use alternate types of weapons. Who would have thought that box cutters could be used to take over an airplane, and how did they get on board?"

Karen couldn't get away from terror, and she needed her sleep. She had some of the sleep aid, Xanax, with her so she took two and eventually drifted off to sleep with the television still blaring. As she drifted off to sleep she reminded herself of the two things necessary to avoid suspicion and questioning by local authorities. First, you must act like you belonged wherever you were. For this you must dress and act the part of a person of status. Second, you had to act as though you were important. Tomorrow they would all dress the part and hopefully look important.

Chapter 29

Athens, Greece
Present Time

Nick ran down the aisle of the airplane and two policemen jumped up from their seats and pointed Uzi submachine guns at him. They shouted something in a language that Nick could not understand and opened fire. Nick felt three slugs enter his body and fell backwards. Then out of nowhere, a very large black crow flew over Nick and shrieked some kind of vague warning. Then the crow flapped its wings erratically, and crashed into the ground.

Nick screamed and startled himself awake. It is strange to hear yourself scream, especially for an ex-Spetsnaz officer. There was nothing he hated more than waking up during a bad dream. Nick had an eerie sense that something was terribly wrong and interrupted this unusual dream to mean that there would be a problem with the airline hijacking.

Nick didn't believe that dreams predict the future, of course, but it was disconcerting and he was a bit superstitious. Dreams do tell about current situations and the current state of your mind. Sometimes non-verbal clues are picked up by the subconscious mind and are examined during dreams, therefore dreams can warn of potential problems. The worried feelings and emotions of his past dreams often lingered with him for hours.

Nick rubbed his eyes and looked at his new twenty-five dollar fake Rolex watch he bought from an Athens' street vendor. It didn't say, "Made in China," but it probably was. The metal watchband was too loose, so the watch dangled down his wrist. He told himself that he would fix it once he got home. The Rolex said that it was past time to get up. He picked up the phone and called Sevorov. It rang and rang and finally he picked up. "Sevorov, Sevorov, wake up. You're wasting the daylight."

"I'm up, comrade," Sevorov answered in a very sleepy voice that belied his statement.

"Are you interested in breakfast?"

"Yes. Meet you downstairs in thirty minutes."

Downstairs, the hotel restaurant had adequate food but nothing special. "That Lesvos Ouzo was too sweet. There is nothing like good Russian vodka," stated Nick.

"Right." Sevorov yawned and took another sip of coffee. "Are you ready for today?"

"Something doesn't feel right."

"What do you mean?"

"I don't know, but I had a dream. I saw that our mission didn't work. I saw failure and saw myself dead."

Sevorov noticed a change in Nick's voice so he gave him his big trademark grin and said, "Don't be like a little sissy girl. Of course we will succeed. Our plans are elegant and simple. No one can defeat us. We are invincible. We cannot fail."

"I know what you are feeling," Sevorov continued. "I know because I also once had doubts. But when you have doubts, remember the slaughtered school children of Beslan. Then get that stupid dream out of your head and get real."

"You are right," said Nick. He sounded surprisingly apologetic. "I'm sorry. I will try to be strong for you. I sometimes need to remember to be real and not pay attention to dreams and feelings. Of course we will win."

"Be strong for yourself, not for me," replied Sevorov in a low voice. "Drink another cup of coffee and finish your breakfast. Then, come back to my room and let's go over the plans for the last time."

Chapter 30

Athens, Greece
Present Time

Karen awoke to her alarm clock and was excited about the prospects of the day. It would be the culmination of almost a year's work and the potential for success looked promising. Karen phoned both Craig and Sevorov, and she was pleased that they were all good to go.

Her ride to the airport only took forty-five minutes, but it was forty-five minutes racked with tension. Karen was in charge of the entire operation, so she was responsible for the plan. Would it work? Was there something she overlooked?

The others all arrived separately by taxicab at The Eleftherios Venizelos International Airport, which is located about 20 miles southeast of Athens in the city of Sparta.

Karen had a ticket on another airline to another destination, but leaving from the same international concourse. Karen got to the airport three hours ahead of time and sat in the lounge looking for anyone who might board Craig's flight early. Any non-crew boarding early would probably be the Saudi equivalent of an air marshal. When she saw him she would write down a description and slip the paper to Sevorov. There was no reliable information of what percent of the Saudi Arabian Airlines flights had air marshals, but it was the Middle East, so the odds are that air marshals are around.

Karen tried to relax by taking deep, slow breaths. Since 9-11, airport surveillance has increased tremendously. There was probably someone, or some camera, watching her now. In today's world, many airports have as many cameras rolling as do gambling casinos, and that is in the hundreds. She didn't want her movement or anxiety to appear to be linked with what would soon happen.

The line was long and Karen had to wait. It was difficult to wait for some searching procedure that you knew would not help against Muslim terror. The Muslim fundamentalist options to destroy a plane are almost limitless. Karen understood why it might be necessary to wait during a doctor's visit. Doctors were very skilled and there are not enough of them compared to the many patients, but to wait for some minimum wage people, whose job is more show than substance, was difficult. Still the rule was wait and that is what she did.

Slowly, very slowly, she inched her way forward towards the screening area. Now only a few people were in front of her. Then it was Karen's turn. She placed the small suitcase on the conveyor and mentally crossed her fingers as it went through the X-rays. The operation was set to go even if the cell phone and Karen did not make it. Still it is much better to have a set of razors on the end of your cane.

The airport security check was not expected to be a major hurdle, but it still made Karen nervous. The wood cane would certainly not be a problem, but the cell phone with the metal rectangle might. Karen personally carried the cell phone from New York to Athens and had no problems. There is no real security when people are allowed to carry lap top computers, radios, CD players and many other metal objects on board.

Karen arranged the cell phone in the carry-on luggage in such a position that the metal rectangle, that broke apart into knives, would be sideways to the x-rays. A regular cell phone battery has a thin metal cover so the view to the operator should be normal. Still the person looking at the carry-on x-rays makes all the difference, so there might still be a problem.

The conveyor operator stopped the belt and Karen held her breath. The operator saw something, but whatever he saw didn't hold his attention. He appeared not to notice any irregularities, and the belt started to move again. The suitcase soon came out of the conveyer. Karen made it. She was in with the cell phone.

Chapter 31

Athens, Greece
Present Time

Sevorov was hunched over and walked with a noticeable limp appearing to be old and feeble. He cowered a little and looked down as he walked through the security checkpoint with the wooden cane. Once through he grunted and pretended to stumble to one side, but before he could fall he recovered his equilibrium. On previous dry runs, the wooden cane and cell phone had been carried through the security screening with no problem. And so it was today. None of the security people noticed, or could have been expected to notice, that beneath the facade of the old gimpy man was a powerful bear.

Craig's scalp prickled with anxiety. Would everything go all right? Would he be able to perform and get his family the money they deserved? Craig's hands were wet and clammy, so he blotted them on his pants. Nervously he walked through the security screening. It was uneventful, even though Craig's voice was not as even as he would have preferred.

All three men have proper documentation, including authentic government issued work permits and entry visas. Since Saudi Arabia is closed to tourists, work permits are essential. Unless you are a Muslim, getting permission to tour Saudi Arabia is almost impossible, but hundreds of non-Muslim workers come and go every day.

Craig and the two Russians each had very good, professionally manufactured, fake passports. These were actual passports, probably stolen from someone, and altered with different numbers and photos.

Karen felt a strange combination of worry and excitement as she saw Sevorov waiting in line with about ten people in front of him. She watched the officials closely examine the passengers in front of Sevorov. She was pleased at the way Sevorov limped forward through the metal detector without incident. Sevorov's cane was in the x-ray conveyer with his small carry-on bag, and no one said a word. After all, it was just a wooden cane like many thousands of others that have come down the conveyer line. Sevorov did a great job of limping like he really needed the cane, and emerged on the other side limping down the concourse on the way to the next line.

Major Sevorov smiled as he handed his passport, plane ticket, and visa to the Greek border official. The name on Major Sevorov's French passport is Maurice J. Duvall. The stone-faced exit official compared the passport photograph to Major Sevorov. The official nodded, stamped the passport and indicated that Major Sevorov could continue towards the waiting area.

The Greek exit officials had no interest in anything except confirming the photographs, stamping the passports, checking the plane tickets and waving people through. Craig and Nick also went through with no difficulties.

Saleh assured Karen that there would be one, but only one, air marshal on the flight, but Karen wondered how he could be so certain. In the waiting area, Karen caught Sevorov's eye and slowly shook her head from side to side. This is the signal there is no sign of an air marshal. This might indicate that there is none on this plane, but it could also mean one or more air marshals could come from another plane and would look just like one of the other passengers. Killing the air marshal would be their first task, but they needed to spot him first.

Karen raised her right arm, stood up and headed to the nearest drinking fountain. Sevorov discretely followed her. Karen put the cell phone on the fountain and when she left, Sevorov picked it up. They were in business.

Chapter 32

Athens, Greece
Present Time

In the airport waiting area, Craig looked around for the two Russians. He tried not to look or act nervous as he pretended to read a paperback novel, but inside his nervous tension was tearing him up. He was a little weak at the knees, much as if he drank too much. He felt a deep sadness for himself and his family. The sadness is mixed with a fear of the fast approaching unknown nightmare.

In the interest of protecting the operation, Craig and the Russians had not previously met or even exchanged pictures. That way, if something happened to the Russians they could not lead an investigation to Craig. Also they would not be able to leak any information that could jeopardize the entire operation.

The Russians saw Craig first when they spotted the blue baseball cap that Craig wore. This was their prearranged signal to identify Craig. They looked at Craig and they made eye contact. Craig of course could hardly miss the large Russian and nodded. There was no verbal communication between the three men. None was necessary, as they all knew their parts in the operation. The men did not get close or move together. Nowadays, there are always cameras and police in airports and they did not want to do anything that appeared the least bit suspicious.

Saudi Arabian Airlines flight SV212 will depart Athens, Greece at 2:30 and arrive in Jeddah, Saudi Arabia at 5:55 in the afternoon. The flight equipment was a McDonnell Douglas MD-90. It has a maximum passenger load of 150 and a configuration of 5 seats across. It has a cockpit crew of 2. This flight was chosen because Craig had experience flying the MD-90. Also, a small plane like this, with a small center aisle, was easier for the two Russians to control than one of the larger jumbo jets with multiple aisles. Additionally, air marshals were more likely to be on the bigger planes rather than the smaller ones.

The two hour wait dragged by, until about twenty minutes prior to the scheduled departing time, the loud speaker finally announced that boarding would begin. As usual, first class seats were called to board first. Craig, Sevorov and Nick boarded the flight on the first call. The sooner they were out of the airport, the less possibility something could go wrong.

As they boarded, Craig scrutinized the cockpit door to determine if it is the old flimsy standard door or a retrofit modern reinforced door. The Russians were relieved when Craig signaled them that it was a weak door, easily broken. If it were a reinforced door, their timetable for storming the cockpit would have to be moved up. They would have to look for their earliest opportunity when the doors first opened, such as when the pilot went to the bathroom or got a cup of coffee from the flight attendant.

If the door never opened, plan B was for Nick to go into a restroom and tear the light fixture off the wall and connect the wires causing a direct short. Then he would put a match to a pile of paper towels he made in the sink and start a fire. The indication of an electrical problem plus the restroom smoke detector was sure to get one of the pilots to open the door and come out of the cockpit to examine the potentially dangerous situation. When the cockpit door opened, Sevorov would have access to get in, but with the un-reinforced doors they were lucky, since it is best to leave storming the cockpit until the best time for that move.

All three men took their seats in the first class section and strapped themselves in. Another reason they boarded early was to look for anyone already on board who might be the Saudi air marshal. Nothing looked suspicious. Sevorov was nervous.

The aircraft taxied out to the end of the runway, and the flight attendant made his rounds, ensuring that everyone had their seat belts properly fastened and their seat backs in the upright position. Nick was relieved when the plane began its taxi down the runway. The engines screamed and the plane's acceleration pushed Nick gently against his seat back. Nick felt his pulse quicken in anticipation of the coming battle, but he began to feel much better now that the plane was actually airborne. His pulse would have sped up much more if he knew how this flight would end, but the die was cast. There was no backing out now.

Sevorov watched the plane lift off and was happy that there were fewer than 100 passengers on board. Karen previously told Sevorov that she planned it so there would be a number of empty seats. She manipulated the passenger levels by purchasing forty-six tickets for a large tour group. There was no tour group so all those seats were considered no-shows. The passenger level was therefore artificially reduced to facilitate their operation. Karen said that the deposit she lost would be well worth it.

Chapter 33

Airborne
Present Time

Once in the air, the flight attendant made his rounds providing coffee, tea and soft drinks. The Russians could use a vodka or two, or three, but Saudi airlines do no serve alcoholic beverages. Craig asked for some milk hoping to settle his stomach, but it didn't work. It only made him visit the rest room every half hour.

First class passengers were served a good-looking seafood dinner, but Craig couldn't eat. He just looked at it and thought that it was his last meal and couldn't even think of eating it. This would not be an easy mission.

Craig squirmed in his chair as he tried to relax. He felt feverish. The plane's air conditioner worked properly, but still beads of perspiration formed on his forehead and spotted his shirt under the armpits. He was so tense that he felt he would explode. "Breathe, just breathe," he told himself. He loosened his seat belt and tried to relax. It seemed like a lifetime ago since the plane took off, but only one hour had passed. The numbers on his digital watch crawled ever so slowly forward.

About two hours into the flight, Craig swallowed a 200mg pill of Provigil. This is the same drug that the U. S. Air Force gives to B-2 bomber pilots who make long-range flights over hostile territory. It would make Craig more alert, but was not supposed to make him nervous. It takes an hour or two for the pill to take maximum effect. He timed it to maximize his alertness when the action started.

After about three hours, Sevorov performed a good act of limping into the restroom. He opened the cell phone and took out the three razor sharp blades from under the battery. He removed the black rubber tip of his hickory wood cane and discarded it in the waste bin.

Next, he mixed the two containers of fast-acting epoxy glue, placing the glue into the three precut groves in the tip of his cane. The groves were designed to lock the blades in, but the glue just makes it stronger. He inserted the blades in the groves and waited a few minutes for the glue to set. This turned the cane into a formidable weapon capable of deadly force. Hickory wood is the same kind of wood used to make ax handles, so it will not break when striking someone.

He then tied a small black plastic bag around the tip of the cane so no one noticed anything, limped back to his seat and nodded to Nick. Nick sat towards the back of the first class section. He was the back-up and reinforcement, should Sevorov need help.

Sevorov knows the moment of action will come shortly, and he sat with rapt attention for any signal from Craig. Craig looked at his stopwatch. The flight from Athens, Greece to Jeddah, Saudi Arabia takes four hours and 25 minutes. The plan was to allow 20 minutes to take over the plane. At the proper time, Craig would stand up and signal plan B. This plan would take into consideration that there might be one, or even two, air marshals aboard the flight.

Craig almost panicked at the thought of the violence ahead. To say he was nervous is a gross understatement. He attempted to clear his mind and swept away the anxieties that drained his energy. He was scared silly, but he keep his mind on business and tried not to think of what might happen.

Craig looked at his watch again. "Almost time," he thought to himself. "Almost, hold on, hold on, and don't rush, a few more minutes. My God, it's time."

Chapter 34

Airborne
Present Time

His heart going like a trip-hammer, Craig swallowed hard and jumped up from his seat and shouted, "Let's go!" to Sevorov who also stood. They walked toward the front of the plane and Craig held his breath as he knocked on the door of the cockpit with that universal code. Knock, knock-knock-knock, knock-knock. The pilot responded to the knock and reached around behind himself and said something in Arabic, and then opened the door a crack.

Sevorov was hunched over and limping, but his muscles were tight and hard. Then, like a snake, he suddenly uncoiled, ready to strike. In a blur of action, Sevorov shoved the door wide open and burst into the cockpit. The battle irrevocably began.

Moving quickly for such a large man, Sevorov used his cane as a spear, thrusting forward off the ball of his right foot. The razors in the tip of the cane sliced the right side of the pilot's neck. In powerful spurts, a geyser of blood spewed from his right carotid artery. It sprayed across the cockpit, splattering the aircraft instrumentation and coloring it red. The pilot tried to move, but his muscles were practically drained of blood. He made some awful gurgling sound and quickly died.

The co-pilot in the right chair saw this and at first remained immobile, staring at the invader. Then, suddenly, he started to move into action. He bend down to reach for something. Pivoting his body with whiplash speed from left to right, Sevorov circled the cane towards the copilot, and with the speed of a striking snake, he caught him in the head. There was a thud as his skull broke audibly under the blow. He immediately lost consciousness, but his body continued to move, jerking and twitching. Sevorov struck him twice more, just to make sure. The co-pilot was dead, but his eyes were still open, and his face had a shocked and terrified look on it.

Both pilots lay motionless in their cockpit chairs. Sevorov reached down and carried the pilot's body from the chair and dumped it on top of the co-pilot. His pulse racing, Craig immediately lowered himself into the pilot's chair to take control of the plane. Blood was everywhere. Blood covered the controls, and Craig felt sick to his stomach from what he just witnessed.

The plane was still on automatic pilot so it continued to fly without any jerking or noticeable change during the killings. It all happened so fast, and with such little noise, that few people could fathom what just took place. Never a religious man, Craig was surprised to hear himself repeating a prayer he learned in church.

Sevorov walked out of the cockpit, shutting the door, and Craig locked it behind him.

Sevorov just stood in front of the cockpit door. He stood straight and powerful, guarding the door. The passengers in first class could tell that something happened. The curtains were closed so the other passengers outside of first class had no clue that anything was wrong. The first class flight attendant must have seen something, because he looked at Sevorov in total disbelief.

For a few long minutes Sevorov continued to stand there until finally the flight attendant approached him and, in Arabic, asked to talk to the pilot. Sevorov did not understand what he said but from his actions Sevorov knew that he must do something. His only thought was to shut him up, and he proceeded to do just that.

Sevorov stepped forward with his right foot, closing the distance between himself and the flight attendant. At the same time, he slammed the flight attendant's head with an upward movement of his powerful right elbow. With a loud bone-crunching sound, the flight attendant's head snapped violently back, exposing the vulnerable extended muscles of the front of his neck. In the same movement, Sevorov curved his right hand downward driving it into the exposed neck and grabbing the windpipe. Twisting his hand he pulled and twisted the windpipe out, easily crushing it. The attendant emitted an awful gurgling, choking sound, twisted in pain, went limp, and crumpled to the floor near the main doorway. Sevorov picked up the lifeless man with a violent jerking motion, swung him around, and deposited him powerfully into one of the first class armchairs. The cane was still in Sevorov's left hand, but he did not need it to silence the unfortunate attendant.

Some of the passengers who witnessed this screamed, and the most dangerous part of the mission began. From the tourist class cabin, a man parted the curtain and walked into first class. "You will raise your hands now," the air marshal announced in Arabic, then he pulled a pistol from his shoulder holster, and flipped the safety forward. "Raise your hands now," he repeated. Sevorov just looked at him, and the man walked closer. Sevorov did not understand the words, but he did understand the threat. He could hear his heart skip a few beats.

The air marshal leveled his Beretta nine-millimeter pistol, aiming directly at Sevorov, and said again, in English this time, "Raise your hands or I will fire!" Sevorov didn't understand English either, and continued to stand in the middle of the aisle. Still, the intent was obvious. As his heart thudded against his ribs, he held his breath and tried to look bewildered. The roar of the nine-millimeter cartridge exploding reverberated through out the plane as a long flash of gunpowder erupted from the gun.

The air marshal was a professional and placed his shots where he was most likely to connect. He aimed at Sevorov's mid-section. It had the greatest margin of success, since it was the largest available target.

The air marshal fired twice in quick succession. The roar from the barrel of the Beretta nine-millimeter pistol echoed throughout the plane and stopped time like a red flag thrown into a football game by the referee. One bullet smacked brutally into the very center of Sevorov's chest. His face twisted in pain and he felt the impact as if it were a kick to his chest. His body jerked backwards, and he fell down, ending face up in the center of the aisle.

The second round struck Sevorov as he fell and hit his left arm. A wave of pain, like a bolt of searing hot lighting, traveled through his wounded arm and he screamed something unintelligible. Blood oozed from Sevorov's left arm, and he staggered, fell and then groaned loudly from the pain.

The enormous explosions of the pistol sounded like a cannon shot as they filled and echoed through the enclosed airplane. The passengers gasped and jumped in their seats. They looked at the air marshal, and then, with open mouths and pale faces, shifted their astonished gaze to Sevorov.

Chapter 35

Airborne
Present Time

Nick glanced around, shifted uneasily in his seat and nervously chewed his lower lip. He could feel his chest pounding and sweat glistened on his forehead and dripped down his face. He looked down at his hands and realized that his knuckles were white from tightly gripping the armrests. "Relax, allow your mind to let go," he told himself. He knew that tension was the enemy of a good marshal artist and he adjusted his body, trying to relax, but it didn't work. The tension was just to great.

Nick raised his right hand to wipe the sweat from his eyes. Every muscle seemed to be as taut as tempered steel. Time slowed and moved with the viscose consistency of molasses. "Follow your instincts," he reminded himself. He scarcely seemed to breathe while his eyes tried to see the best time to commit to action. Then suddenly, it was time.

Nick was already tensed to stand. He took a deep breath, his pulse quickened, and he quietly leaped to his feet. Nick was only a few rows behind the air marshal, who still faced Sevorov. The air marshal didn't have a clue what was happening behind him. Being careful not to make any unexpected sounds, Nick quickly moved forward until he was about a foot from the air marshal.

Like lightning, Nick reached up and his hands shot out. He positioned his hands on the air marshal's head. One of his hands grabbed the chin, and the other hand grabbed the back of the head. With one quick motion, Nick pulled his hands in opposite directions. He twisted the head just as he had been taught and, sure enough, it worked. He felt the air marshal's neck vertebrae resist the torque for a very short moment, but then with a loud crack, the vertebrae gave way and snapped the spinal cord. With very little effort, Nick broke his neck.

The air marshal's gun fell out of his right hand and hit the floor with a thump and soft clatter. There was a choking gasp as his face contorted itself into shock and disbelief. His lips drew back from his teeth, and his mouth twisted itself into a scream. He released a soundless scream and then died. His body went instantly limp and fell vertically down, ending face up on the cabin floor. His face had a look of shock, and his mouth remained open.

"Damn! It worked!" thought Nick. This was obviously not one of those moves you could practice to completion with your workout partner. Until this moment, Nick was not sure he could actually kill someone with his bare hands using this simple movement. His teachers were right. You don't need a gun to win. If you practice something over and over again, when the time comes, you don't think, you just do it, and you do it right.

All eyes were on Nick as he hurriedly picked up the air marshal's gun and walked over the body to the front of the plane. He bent down to examine Sevorov and was relieved to see him move. Brimming with a sense of success, Sevorov started to get up and slowly rose to his haunches, and then staggered to his feet. The body of the air marshal remained in the aisle as an obstacle to anyone else who was brave enough to come forward.

The bullet had struck Sevorov in the chest, blowing him backward and knocking him down. However, he was not seriously hurt, since his Colombian body armor had no trouble stopping the underpowered slug that air marshals use in a crowded airplane. The special ammo is similar to presidential rounds used by the Secret Service. They are meant to put someone down, but still not be powerful enough to go completely through his body and hit someone else. In an airplane you didn't want the ammo destroying vital electrical wires or hydraulic lines that could crash the plane.

The left arm wound caused shooting pains, and made his large triceps hurt as if they were on fire, but it was not a serious wound. The bullet only went through his muscle and missed the bone and artery. Ignoring his pain, Sevorov rose to his haunches and then stood erect. He grabbed his cane and again resumed control over the airplane. The danger and pain, and most of all the glory of successful action, made him feel especially alive.

Sevorov had purposely played dead to trick the air marshal to come close enough so that Nick would be behind him. With his cane, and the now the Beretta nine millimeter, the Russians knew that they would succeed and were in command of the situation. If there were another air marshal, he would now face a firefight. More passengers, their eyes wide with fear, screamed and ran for shelter to the back of the plane, but no new air marshal came forward.

Chapter 36

Airborne
Present Time

Craig just witnessed the unbelievably quick murder of the pilot and the copilot. Blood from the pilot had spattered everywhere in the cockpit, and also on Craig. He swallowed hard, felt a cold chill climb up his spine, and his body started shaking. Large red splotches appeared on his cheeks and terror tightened his stomach muscles. He felt as if someone had grabbed his stomach in a vice-like grip and squeezed until he just knew he would vomit. There was no barf bag in sight, so Craig leaned to the side, and the contents of his stomach splashed onto the cockpit floor.

Craig was extremely nervous and upset. His heart was beating incredibly fast, and he could barely breathe. He couldn't get the sight of the killing out of his mind, and the bodies were right next to him. It seemed that the reek of death saturated the cockpit.

Craig suddenly realized that he did not want to die. Only this morning he thought that he was ready to welcome death as a way to escape the terrible pain and suffering, yet now, instead of resigning himself to death, he panicked, but he knew that it was way too late, that this was his only chance to redeem himself, and that he must go through with his agreement.

For a few moments, his heart sank within him, and he felt extremely depressed. He squeezed his lips together into a tight grimace and held his breath. He clutched his hands tightly into fists to get control of his shaking. He knew he had to get ahold of himself. He knew he had to think and take control of his own thoughts.

It took all of Craig's courage, but he recovered his resolve and managed to get himself under control. Even though he was half crazy with fear, he somehow felt more alive than he had been since learning of his illness.

As his rapid breathing slowed, and as his heartbeat decelerated, he remembered the importance of his mission. He switched off the automatic avionics and programmed the GPS unit. The GPS device began blinking. This meant the plane was off course.

He slowly turned east thirteen degrees and the GPS device stopped blinking. They were on target for 21°25.64 north latitude and 39°48.89 east longitude. Craig knew that the course that lay ahead would be very difficult, but he also knew that he was now on the way to fulfill his destiny.

"Saudi Arabia flight SV212," demanded the radio in Arabic. "You are off course. Please respond." Craig ignored it but kept the radio on. Craig didn't speak Arabic so it was better to keep radio silence until he got a chance to take out his tape player.

The McDonnell Douglas MD-90 was familiar to Craig, and he flew it as easily as driving a car. Still, Craig had never been so close to gory death before. He could still feel his heart pounding in his throat. He felt a wetness on him, and then realized that he wet his pants without even knowing it. Even in his Air Force days, the carnage below was always far away on the ground and impersonal, and Craig was high in the sky just doing his job.

He never shared a small room with two dead bodies. Craig looked away disgusted and indignant; but his indignation was neutralized by his astonishment at this incomprehensible brutality. "God!" he begged out loud, "I am a sick man. It isn't fair to ask me to end my life this way." There was no answer.

"Get a grip on yourself," he said and tried to focus all his mental energy on the task of performing his mission.

Craig was tense and worried about the plan going badly. After all, no operation was ever fully planned. Things always go wrong. Craig was prepared to die, but the thought of somehow being captured and tortured put goose bumps on his neck. Craig could not take pain. After all, that was why he elected to die here. He was aware of a sick taste in his mouth, but soldiered on.

"Saudi Arabia flight SV212," demanded the radio in Arabic again. "You are off course. Please respond."

Craig took out his small portable tape player, held it close to the microphone and pushed the play button. He pushed the airplane talk button; the tape played to the Saudi Air Route Traffic Control Center. In Arabic it said that they were working on an electrical power problem, and that the plane would return to the airport. There was no immediate danger. The message repeated itself, and then Craig let go of the talk button. This pre-recorded message was meant to confuse and deceive the traffic control center so that they would hesitate before sending fighters to investigate. Since the flight would be in the air no more than an extra fifteen minutes, a few minutes of deception was all they needed.

Chapter 37

Airborne
Present Time

Arabic shouting came from the tourist section of the plane. Several men stood in the aisle and walked forward. Other Arabs joined them and their number was now at least a dozen. They slowly moved into first class and continued shouting. They began chanting something. "Allah Ackbar, Allah Ackbar, Allah Ackbar," They repeated it over and over and continued their advance.

Sevorov and Nick were prepared for this eventuality. Their plan indicated there would be up to six high level terrorists on this plane. That, after all, was the reason for the hijacking. The plan took into account that these terrorists might not be captured willingly, and would possibly try to retake the plane. Still, it looked like there were over a dozen men advancing on them. The terrorists must have been able to convince others to join them.

Nick carefully surveyed the plane's passengers. For the first time in his life, he noted his hands shaking. Nick checked the Beretta's magazine and quickly counted the rounds. It was not fully loaded and had only six of the nine-millimeter hollow point rounds in the magazine and one in the chamber. There could be a problem, especially if there was a second air marshal on the plane. Sevorov quickly but carefully assessed his position. He thought they could be over run if enough people charged them at once.

"Wait for my order before shooting," said Sevorov in a loud whisper, that sounded almost like the hiss of a rattlesnake's tongue. "Be ready to fire. You can't miss at this distance. When I say fire, give them a volley and make every shot count. It's our only chance, for they'd surely overwhelm us if their charge succeeds." Sevorov moved a few steps forward, taking a position in front of Nick.

The passengers were now within range of the cane, so Sevorov flicked the cane out in crossing motions. The closest passenger was a hatchet-faced man in a gray shirt and a typical Muslim terrorist beard. Sevorov swung the cane downward striking the Muslim's head and he fell to his knees, but did not go all the way down. Sevorov then whipped the cane up, striking him under his chin. His teeth clacked loudly and his head snapped back, knocking him down in the center of the aisle. As Sevorov did this, he let out a tremendous deep and loud shout. These martial arts' yells serve to concentrate the blow and make it more powerful, but for a huge and strong man like Sevorov, his reason for shouting was not to get more power. This was meant to scare the daylights out of the passengers with the terrible howling battle cry of a warrior prepared to kill in mortal combat.

Humans have an instinctive fear of a large animal with a loud deep growl. In nature, the lower the growl the bigger the animal, so Sevorov shouted as deeply as he could, and it worked. The passengers stopped advancing and Sevorov charged them now swinging his cane from side to side and knocking down another passenger.

One man continued to charge, and Sevorov knocked him down with a quick blow to his head. The blow struck his jaw and knocked his head toward the left. His lower jaw hung strangely down. He hit the deck screaming in pain. Sevorov thrust the razor augmented tip of the cane into his neck, but he continued to scream. Sevorov thrust again and this time there was blood and silence.

Now anguished oaths in Arabic came from the back of the plane and other Muslims joined the charge. Sevorov waited until the nearest Muslims were not more than five feet away. Then in an extremely loud voice, Sevorov shouted, "Nick, fire! Now! Now! Shoot the rag head, baby killers!" He moved immediately to the left to get out of the way.

Nick braced himself against the airplane's motion with his left hand holding a seat back. He raised his right hand and opened up with the nine millimeter.

Nick didn't aim through the sites. In combat shooting, if the range is less than twenty feet, he was taught to just raise the pistol and use the outline of the entire gun to line up the target. Using the sights of the pistol for close-up shooting would have been too slow.

For Nick it was an eerie feeling, but these were no longer people charging at him. They were just targets. The first round ripped into the closest man's stunned face. He immediately sank to his knees and then fell backwards until he was staring up at a ceiling.

The loud reverberating sound of pistol fire cannot be mistaken for anything else. The noise was especially deafening in the enclosed airplane, and the passengers froze in their tracks. The nine-millimeter fired again, and the closest man arched backward, blood spurting from his forehead. The nine-millimeter fired once more and the next closest man's chest discharged a crimson spray of blood. He fell backward and collapsed onto the aisle.

The nine-millimeter fired again and again; passengers continued to fall down. Frantic screams and shouts rang out from all over the terrified plane. Two of the shots missed their marks. Nick found out that combat shooting in a moving airplane with people running and shouting is not as easy as target practice on the firing range.

After the sixth shot Sevorov barked, "Advance! Move forward! Close and kill!" They both took a few steps towards the passengers. Sevorov swung his cane, striking anyone within range, and Nick fired his last shot.

In less than a minute, seven passengers lay dead or dying. Pools of red blood slowly spread from their wounds. Some lay motionless, obviously dead, or soon to be. Two cried out and begged for help. The rest of the passengers surged backward in quick retreat.

Their courage gave way when they saw their fellow passengers dying all around them. Most of them had never seen this amount of carnage and death before. Their faces pale with fear, they fled to the back of the airplane, away from the gunfire.

Chapter 38

Airborne
Present Time

One of the passengers in the rear of the plane was able to make cell phone contact with an emergency operator on the ground. He described the bloodbath in the airplane. "This is unbelievable," he said. "Two non-Arab infidels are in the front of the airplane and just killing everyone. One is really big and the other is average. Somehow they were able to get guns on board the plane. I don't know what we can do. I think there must be at least ten people dead. This one really big guy is killing people with a stick."

"What are the pilots doing?" was the reply from the ground.

"I don't know. The last thing the pilots said was that they had an electrical power problem. I haven't heard or seen the pilots since the shooting began. I'm hiding behind a seat near the very back of the plane. I hope they don't see me. One of their shots put a hole in the wall behind me, and I don't know where it went after that. I hope it didn't damage anything that will make us crash."

"What are the demands of the people with the guns? What are they saying over the public address system?"

"They didn't say anything. We're all scared."

"Try to relax and don't fight them. I'm sure they will have some demands."

"We don't know what to do. Some of the passengers want to attack them again. There are only two of them. One of the passengers says they may be out of ammunition."

"I can't believe this is happening to you. What can I do to help?"

"Call the police or call the Saudi Arabian Airline and tell them that it's Saudi Arabia flight SV212 from Athens, Greece to Jeddah, Saudi Arabia."

"Did you hear me? Hello? Hello?" The cell phone lost its signal, and the passenger pushed its buttons trying to acquire another signal, but he was unable to find one.

Another passenger was also on his cell phone talking to a relative. "I think they've taken over the cockpit," he cried. "I saw a lot of people on the floor, and I think they are dead. There is screaming coming from the first class section. I am scared and don't know what to do."

"It will be all right. I am sure that terrorists would not harm a Muslim," was the response.

"The plane is making strange moves. I also heard an announcement that there was a bomb on board. Phone Saudi Arabia Airlines and tell them to help us."

"Stay calm. Terrorists do not attack Muslims. You will be all right. They are probably going after an infidel on board. Don't worry. Allah will protect you."

The call lasted about two minutes, after which the relative tried unsuccessfully to contact Flight SV212.

A few minutes passed, and the passengers continued to regain their composure. They began regrouping and again chanting. First only a few chanted, but the chanting broke the tension. Now many others joined in.

One of the wounded passengers was in extreme pain. The sound he released was barely human. It was a loud wailing cry that everyone on the airplane heard. Another wounded passenger joined in the wailing. The cries for help from these two wounded passengers resulted in still more people in the back of the plane joining the chants of, "Allah Ackbar, Allah Ackbar, Allah Ackbar."

Seeing this, Sevorov decided to make an example of the wounded to scare the passengers. He gave one of his most powerful martial blood curdling screams and swung his cane loudly striking one wounded man solidly on the head. Then he thrust at the man's neck with his razor tipped cane slicing through his windpipe. He died immediately, and the other wounded man gasped but stopped shouting.

Some of the passengers saw this and instead of quieting them down it only upset them more. They chanted louder and louder as if getting their courage up to attack.

One of the Muslims emerged as a leader and managed to get some of the passengers under some semblance of control. They quickly devised a strategy of attack.

As they came forward, they opened the overhead bins and grabbed suitcases. They would use the suitcases as shields from the bullets and the cane during their next charge. The carry-on suitcases were not big and afforded only minimal shields, but still, they gave the passengers some protection and a sense of optimism and bravery that they could retake the plane.

Sevorov knew Nick was out of ammo and his mind raced trying to find answers. They might not be able to withstand the next charge. Things were looking worse and worse every second. Again the passengers began moving towards the Russians. Their numbers increased and now there were more than two dozen of them. They made their way forward through the aisle littered with the bodies of the recent carnage.

Chapter 39

Saudi Arabia
Present Time

The Jeddah, Saudi Arabia air route traffic controller was aware that something was wrong with Saudi Arabian flight SV212. They weren't on their flight path and continued flying well past the airport. Additionally, after the message about the electrical power problem, flight SV212 did not respond to repeated attempts at radio contact. This could be explained by electrical problems, but the traffic controller's radar continued to observe flight SV212 flying quickly away from the Jeddah airport, and it was losing altitude. This rang alarms in the control tower, but there was still no hint of a hijacking.

Then the panicked phone call came in from Ali Al-Akkad. "My son is returning home on flight SV212, and he said the plane has been hijacked!"

The traffic controller cleared his throat and tried to sound relaxed, "Tell me exactly what he said."

"As I said to the other man, my son is on flight SV212 and called me from his cell phone. Two non-Arabs are in the front of the airplane and killing people. They both have guns, and some of their shots put holes through the airplane walls."

"Don't worry, Mr. Al-Akkad; we will take care of it from here. Thank you for calling us."

During the phone call, flight SV212 got so low that it disappeared from the radar screens. All hell broke loose as the air traffic controllers spread the word of the hijacking and called for help. The most important call was to the Royal Saudi Air Force.

Saudi Arabia has 5 of the E-3 AWAC airborne warning and control system planes with down-looking radar capabilities. They are able to acquire airplanes that are too low for ground radar to detect. One of the AWACs was airborne and in less than a minute relayed the position of the missing airline. It was still on the same track that it had previously been on before it disappeared from the ground radar.

A flight of two F-15 Eagles from Taif Air Force Base was on a routine patrol. The flight was only about 95 miles from the intercept point and was redirected to intercept Saudi Arabian SV212. The F-15

Eagles were armed with intercept missiles and are capable of supersonic Mach 2.5 speeds, so they could be on target in less than five minutes.

Chapter 40

Airborne
Present Time

The two Russians were near the body of the dead air marshal still lying in the aisle. "Search him for more ammo," shouted Sevorov in Russian as he continued to swing his cane at anyone in sight. Nick bent down and dug through the dead man's pockets. Wallet, a set of keys, pocket change, and then he saw the gun holster. It had a front compartment that contained another full nine-millimeter magazine. Nick dropped the empty magazine to the floor, rammed the full one up the grip of his Berretta, and let the bolt chamber the first round. They were back in business, and a lesson had to be taught.

This time Nick took careful aim and began shooting. The head of the closest Muslim snapped back as the bullet pierced his right eye. The force of the impact knocked him violently backwards and down on the floor. Blood spurted from the pulsing wound in his head, but it turned to a trickle as he quickly died.

Nick shot six times and six passengers fell. The plane was filled with hysteria and loud discordant sounds of screams and gunfire. Nicks every movement was super tense and more alive than anything else he ever felt in life. He quickly adjusted to the boom of the pistol in the enclosed plane, and the screams of the wounded. He was now a well-trained killing machine and did his job expertly. One shot, one kill, and in less that a minute the passengers again retreated to the back of the plane. For the first time since the baby killers slaughtered the school children in Beslan, Russia, Nick felt a release. He relaxed, but maybe too soon.

His seventh shot ricocheted off a suitcase and went astray, hitting a window. The stray shot obliterated the windowpane creating the noise of forcefully escaping air. Sevorov saw this and worried that the plane might crash.

If the plane were at a higher elevation there may have been a greater problem, but the McDonnell Douglas MD-90 was designed to retain adequate air pressure even with one window blown away at high altitude. At the low level they were now at, there was no problem. However, the blown out window did succeed in shocking the passengers. The rushing sound of air escaping made the hearts of the passengers sink down into their shoes. This succeeded even more than the gunfire in quieting them down.

The gun Nick captured made everything easier. Except for the unlucky air marshal, the passengers were unarmed. They were never a real threat. They had probably never before participated in a life or death battle, but Sevorov was a combat soldier. He had killed before, and for him killing was a natural thing to do. He was so well-trained that he did not moralize. He did not even think. He just killed.

Chapter 41

Airborne
Present Time

Craig forced himself not to pay attention. He could hear the gunfire and the shouting behind his back but resolved to ignore it. Then his aircraft radio came to life. "Saudi Arabia flight SV212 this is Saudi Air Route Traffic Control Center in Jeddah. Please answer. Saudi Arabia flight SV212 it is imperative that you answer." There was no response.

"Saudi Arabia flight SV212 this is Saudi Air Route Traffic Control Center in Jeddah. Be advised that a squadron of Saudi Air Force F-15s has been dispatched to intercept your flight. You are required to land at the nearest runway immediately." The original message was in Arabic, but it was repeated in English.

Craig took out his small portable tape player for the second time, held it close to the microphone and pushed the play button. He pushed the talk button, and the tape played to the Saudi Air Route Traffic Control Center. In Arabic it said that they had an electrical power problem and that the plane would return to the airport. All passengers are fine and not in danger.

Craig scanned the skies for fighter planes but saw none. Still, in a passenger jet you cannot see much to your rear. Also fighters flew so fast they could still appear from any direction at a moment's notice.

If a jet fighter appeared, Craig would get on the radio and begin calling, "Mayday, Mayday!" This is the internationally recognized distress call for aircraft of all nations. This would buy him some time. But his best bet for now was to descend to a lower altitude so that the radar would not detect him and be able to direct the fighters to his location.

The plan depended on the belief that there would not be enough time for Saudi officials to quantify the threat, scramble fighter jets, and intercept the passenger jet.

Chapter 42

Airborne
Present Time

Craig was painfully aware of the continuing commotion in the passenger compartment. His heart beat fast and he knew that the next few minutes would be decisive. He exhaled and momentarily shut his eyes. He prayed that the Russians would prevail and get control. If not, he would have a real problem. The one thing Craig could not take is pain, like from torture. If someone started hurting him, he knew he could not hold out and would land the plane wherever they demanded. But the shooting stopped, and Craig felt a sigh of relief. He had other things to keep him busy without a passenger revolt.

Craig continued his descent to escape radar, and had already passed through 1,000 feet. The plane headed lower as if getting ready to land. Sevorov had been told that the plane would have to fly low to escape radar detection, and that they would fly only a few hundred feet above the ground. At 700 feet the plane burst through a few low scattered clouds, and the ground became fully visible. The sun was now starting to set, and soon it would slide behind the hills. To Craig, the declining sun was a symbol of the decline and end of his life.

The city of Mecca is situated on an inclined valley surrounded by barren hills, and very small mountains. Mecca is only fifty miles from their scheduled destination of Jeddah, Saudi Arabia. In an airplane it's only minutes away, and from the cockpit, Craig could already see the first far away outline of the buildings in the city of Mecca.

The city quickly grew larger, and now Craig saw the unique outline of the great Mosque of Mecca and braced for what he knew would be the final few minutes of his life. He did not lower his slats and flaps as planes normally do prior to landing. They would slow the plane and give too much lift. Craig wanted to approach quickly and impact with the maximum amount of force. The more force, the greater the damage to the mosque. The plane was a little high, so he lowered the nose a bit. The plane's automatic warning system blared "Danger, losing altitude. Pull up! Pull up!"

The plane was very close to the target located at 21°25.64 north latitude and 39°48.89 east longitude. Craig now saw the large black cube building called the Kaaba. That was ground zero, and he was amazed that the plane was exactly on target. All those years as a pilot taught him the skills for precision flying. He knew that he was finishing the work that the terrorists had begun back on September eleventh.

Chapter 43

Airborne
Present Time

Suddenly two Saudi Air Force F-15s appeared in front of Craig's aircraft and rolled their wings indicating that Craig should follow them and land. Craig saw that they were fully armed with air-to-air missiles under their wings, and knew they could easily shoot him down.

At this point Craig had nothing to lose. He was less than a minute from the target, and he knew the F-15s would hesitate to shoot down a passenger jet over a crowded city. If they would just hesitate another thirty seconds, it would be too late to stop him.

Except for the recorded message, Craig had kept radio silence, but now keyed the microphone and spoke in French. He does not speak French, but memorized the message that would be sure to tell the world why the plane was hijacked. "Mayday, Mayday! Tower this is flight SV 212. Over. Tower, we can not hear you! T-3, I repeat, T-3. Code 13. Code 13. Respond. Over." Craig was hopeful that this message, in French, would confuse the control tower and F-15s allowing him the few seconds of time that he needed.

The McDonnell Douglas MD-90 had only about a fifth of its fuel remaining. The long trip from Athens used up the rest. To maximize the damage to the target below, Craig would increase his air speed. He angled the plane towards the ground and accelerated to its top speed of over six hundred knots.

The change in the plane's speed and the increased down angle alerted some of the passengers. One of the passengers looked out the window to try and determine where the plane was heading. One look and the blood drained from his face. Every muscle in his body tensed as he shouted, "We are flying low. We are flying very, very low. We are flying way too low." Seconds later he screamed in Arabic, "Oh my God we are way too low."

Other passengers now looked out the windows and saw they were getting dangerously close to the ground and flying very fast. The wrenching horror of the gunfire and killing aboard the MD-90 aircraft was surpassed by the even greater horror of its speedy terminal plunge towards the ground. Pointing their fingers out the windows, some of them started screaming.

Sevorov's gut told him something was wrong. He moved a dead passenger out of the way and looked out a nearby window. He expected to see the plane flying low to avoid radar. What he saw stopped his breathing in mid-breath.

A sudden wave of worry nibbled at his mind. It occurred to him that the plane flew way too low. "Wait a minute. Wait a minute," he thought. Worried thoughts flickered through his brain so fast that only a second later he realized that he had to do something.

Sevorov knocked loudly on the cockpit door that Craig had locked. There was no answer so Sevorov pounded real hard on it. Still there was no answer.

"Think!" he told himself. He had to think of what to do and he had to act now.

Sevorov snapped an order to Nick, "Stay here and guard the door."

Sometimes people realize more than they realize. This was one of those times. Sevorov sensed something and was now really worried. Sevorov gripped the knob of the cockpit door and tried to turn it. The door would not open.

With all the strength he could summon, Sevorov hurled his body against the cockpit door throwing his full weight into the push. He made contact with his right shoulder, and with his enormous strength, he easily broke the flimsy door open.

Bursting through to the cockpit, his eyes bulged in horror. As if his mind was in slow motion, Sevorov stared out the cockpit window in open-mouthed shock. The airplane was going awfully fast, way too fast. It was very low to the ground and getting lower. And the biggest shock of all, a Saudi F-15 fighter plane, flew only fifty yards in front of them, rolling its wings.

Sevorov was not easily frightened. He survived many firefights without being frightened. In fact, the last time he had been frightened was when he was fired from the Russian Army by General Gennady Troshev. But when Sevorov looked at the disaster that loomed in front of his eyes, a shudder of horror ran through his body. For the first time since being shot, the cold powerful rage within Sevorov diminished and was replaced with utter shock and disbelief.

Sevorov assumed that Craig was trying to evade the Saudi F-15 fighter and was flying dangerously low to do this. But how could you evade a fighter? For a moment he experienced a raw terror that paralyzed him. Through sheer will power, he shook the emotion off and got back to action.

"Pull up! Pull up! Pull up now," said Sevorov in Russian and then again in French. His mouth was so dry from fear that the words were more whispers than shouts. Craig didn't seem to hear. The wailing cockpit alarms, and the sight of the second F-15 on the right side of their plane, confirmed to Sevorov that the aircraft was doomed.

Sevorov swallowed hard. In the past, he had seen death in many forms. During periods of his battles against Muslim fundamentalists, scarcely a day had passed without that sad experience. But it had never seemed as horrifying or uncanny as at this moment. He didn't want to die. He wanted to do something, but he didn't know what to do. Maybe Craig could lose the F-15s by flying so low. But the airplane was heading even lower. How low was too low?

The plane was so close to impact that there was nothing Sevorov could do even if he knew what to do, but he had no idea what to do. He was just a spectator to an impending disaster, his own disaster.

Sevorov felt helpless. He did not know how to fly a plane. He couldn't kill the only live pilot on the plane. His mind whirled, but still there was no answer. He was stuck. There was no time. His thoughts were confused because there was no immediate solution to his dilemma. His mind whirled back to his childhood, to his parents, his wife and children.

The plane was only seconds from the target, and it quickly came up and filled the cockpit window. An impotent primal rage came over Sevorov. He snapped out of his confusion and screamed and swore in Russian. He let out an ear shattering curse, not a cry of anguish, but one of utter boiling undirected rage.

The cry startled Craig. He knew he should have felt a rush of pure panic. But he didn't feel any. He knew exactly where he was and he knew he was going to die.

The target became blurry as Craig's eyes filled with tears. Everything seemed to be in slow motion. Craig didn't feel the disaster and death of the impending crash but somehow for the first time in his life, he sensed a spiritual rapture in the unfolding events. All at once, Craig had a feeling that everything would be all right. He knew that this would be a good death.

For most of his life Craig had no real religion. Still, as a small boy, he was raised by his mother with strong Catholic spiritual values. It was not surprising, then, that a prayer from his childhood would flash into his mind at this time.

His last coherent thoughts before impact were the words of a prayer he learned long ago in childhood, "Now I lay me down to sleep. I pray the Lord my soul to keep." A feeling of relief surrounded Craig like a warm, relaxing bath.

Chapter 44

Mecca, Saudi Arabian
Present Time

Saudi Arabian Airlines flight SV212 was almost perfectly flown. It made contact with the right side of the top half of the large black cube-shaped building called the Kaaba, located inside the Sacred Mosque of Mecca. There was a blinding flash and the sound was deafening and reverberated throughout the plane. Craig lurched forward as the plane smashed into the Kaaba. Then, there was nothing but death.

Fuel from the plane set everything on fire. The explosion and fireball lit up the horizon and could be seen from almost anywhere in the city of over one million inhabitants. People on the ground pointed and looked up at the fireball and thick smoke. They tried to determine where it originated. Then the sound of the explosion startled those who did not yet see the fireball. The airliner crashed into the Kaaba with such devastating force that the sound was heard throughout the city of Mecca.

"Saudi Arabia flight SV212," demanded the control tower in Arabic. "You are off our radar. Please respond. Repeat, please respond." There was no response and there was no one left alive.

This was not a normal crash where the airplane has slowed down and then crashes and skids along the ground resulting in large sections of the airplane still intact. This was a crash, at full speed, into a very large and solid structure, resulting in maximum damage.

An hour later, after the smoke cleared, part of the right wing of the McDonnell Douglas MD-90 was all that was left that looked like it was once an airplane. The rest of the plane merged with the Kaaba into an inferno and was consumed in the intense fire.

About half of the Kaaba was totally demolished and smoke and steam still rose from what was left of it. Sirens and revolving red light pulsed in the night. Ambulances, fire trucks, police cars, and other vehicles rushed as many as 600 dead and injured to hospitals in frenzied convoys that careened through the streets of Mecca.

Streams of white chemical foam arced over the burning Kaaba. Firefighters moved back and forth spraying water on stubborn hot spots, but were hampered by the lack of adequate water pressure from the far away fire hydrants. Paramedics and other medical workers and an army of various security men rushed back and forth attending to the wounded. The city was in almost total panic as it contemplated the unprecedented violence and death.

This infrastructure of the city was not prepared for this level of destruction, and coping with the disaster was at first impossible. The thought of the Kaaba sustaining this level of disaster was beyond the imagination of the Muslim population.

Chapter 45

Paris, France
Present Time

Fours hours ago, while Sevorov, Nick, and Craig were boarding their plane, Karen waited to board her plane to Paris. It was time for an identity shift to confuse any cameras that may have recorded her presence. She went to the ladies' room and then entered one of the toilet stalls. There she took off the business sport coat and replaced it with a faded blue sweatshirt that she got from her carry-on luggage. Next, she put on a shoulder length brown wig and a pair of uncorrected wire-rimmed glasses. When she exited the ladies' room the conservative businesswoman was no more. She had been replaced by a new woman with long hair and glasses.

Karen's plane departed about two hours after Craig and the Russians and she arrived at the Charles de Gaulle Airport in Paris. She glanced at her watch and calculated that, if all went well, this was about the same time as the Saudi Arabian Airlines would crash into the Sacred Mosque of Mecca.

Now in Paris, she proceeded to the airport storage lockers where she had previously stored her suitcase. She retrieved it and carried it to the arriving area where she hailed a taxi.

In her large suitcase was a laptop with prewritten news releases, as well as names and e-mail addresses of the editors of some major news organizations. Also in the case were a new identity card, a passport, and credit cards. Karen would return to New York tomorrow using a new identity, just in case she was under any suspicion.

Karen grabbed a taxi and rode down a broad boulevard past gatherings of Parisians strolling down the sidewalks and chatting around outdoor café tables. She had the taxi drop her at a hotel off Saint-Germain Boulevard, about four blocks from her real hotel. She knew this hotel had Wi-Fi computer access for guests to use in conducting their business. She found a comfortable sofa, fired up her notebook and sent her teaser e-mail to her pre-selected contact list. The e-mail just advised the various news media to stay tuned for the big story she would send them tomorrow about the attack in Mecca. It was signed the T-3 group. This advance e-mail would establish the authenticity of the e-mail she would send after the attack was news.

Karen then walked the four blocks to her hotel. Upon checking into her hotel room, she turned on the radio, scanning through all the stations. She anxiously looked for news about Saudi Arabia. Any news this quick was really too much to hope for, but Karen kept scanning. Finally, there it was. Speaking in French, the newscaster said, "An incomplete report from an independent source said there was an accidental airplane crash near the Saudi Arabian city of Mecca. There are reports of some deaths and injuries."

Karen continued scanning the television and radio for news. More accurate news coverage was lacking since the only press allowed in Mecca is the Saudi Arabia controlled media. A few hours after the crash, spokesmen for the Saudi Arabia Government in Riyadh declined to comment, except to say that there was a tragic airplane crash.

More hours passed. It was after midnight before the Saudi National Television announced, "Yesterday a plane crashed into the Great Mosque of Mecca and damaged the Kaaba. There is an indication that the crash might have been caused by terrorists. Little more is known at this time, but we will keep you informed."

This was a moment to be savored, and a huge joyful grin spread across Karen's face. "Oh, yes! Oh, yes!" she shouted to herself. Karen knew she had succeeded even beyond her most optimistic dreams. She was overcome by the pride of accomplishment.

She felt like celebrating and left her hotel. She walked happily along the pavement flanking the tree-lined boulevard towards a nearby bar and bought a bottle of their best Cabernet Sauvignon wine. She returned to the hotel and poured herself a glass. She utterly relaxed in the warm glow of the wine. It felt like a post-stress reaction. This is the first time she really relaxed in a great many weeks. Not once has she stopped planning and thinking and just sipped a bottle of good wine like she did tonight. It was as if her body said that now is the time to restore her sanity and peace of mind. That night Karen slept the deep, perfect, death-like sleep of victory that only someone who had risked everything and won could possibly understand.

The next morning Karen woke early, still feeling great about the successful mission, and anxious to hear the latest news. But first she put on her white gloves, to avoid leaving fingerprints, and walked down the street to another nearby hotel that had a few computers set up for guests to send e-mail. Since she was early, there were no other people in the computer room and she inserted the CD and copied it to her yahoo account and sent all the e-mails. The expanded full headers would show the e-mail was sent from an originating IP address at this hotel in Paris, France, but there would be no connection to Karen.

Chapter 46

Various Locations
Present Time

The television coverage was slow in reporting the Mecca attack. The Saudis do not have freedom of the press, and only Muslims are allowed in Mecca. Additional time was lost in the editing and censoring of the video footage of the crash aftermath.

Radio accounts of the events came more quickly. "Saudi Arabian Airlines flight SV212 crashed in Mecca this evening at about 6:05 PM. There were 77 passengers and 4 crew members on board. It was a catastrophic crash, and it is believed that there are no survivors. Witnesses told authorities that the plane flew very low before it crashed. It was reported that there had been distress signals and indications of trouble from the crew before the plane went down."

"Muhammad Yusuf Ali, a spokesman for the airlines said that several theories were being explored, including pilot error, bad weather along the flight routes, low-quality fuel, or terrorist acts. A spokesman for Eleftherios Venizelos International Airport said all proper pre-flight procedures had been followed."

It was almost one in the morning when the video news came and was fed to international news sources. It said there was an accident and that a plane had crashed into the Kaaba in Mecca and many hundreds of people were killed or injured.

The Associated Press scooped the other news groups with some great background on the disaster in Mecca. AP got it first, but during the next hour all the networks were live with similar reports: "Hundreds of bodies of crash victims were recovered at the great Mosque of Mecca where Saudi Arabian Airlines flight SV212 crashed. The Great Mosque of Mecca is the oldest and most sacred building in Islam."

"Inside the huge courtyard of the Sacred Mosque is a large, 45 foot tall, black building called the Kaaba. It is the most sacred shrine in all of Islam. It is a windowless cube-shaped building with a flat roof near the center of the Great Mosque in Mecca. It is built of grey basalt stone blocks and covered with gold-embroidered black cloth."

"Muslims everywhere in the world turn toward the Kaaba when they pray. Visiting the Kaaba is the chief goal of the required pilgrimage of Muslims. The Islamic faithful run and walk around it seven times, praying and reciting verses from the Koran. It is the most sacred spot in all of Islam."

"The Kaaba is empty inside except for one corner where the Black Stone is housed. This stone is called the Hajr-al-aswad, and it is a heavy oval stone of reddish black color. Its diameter is about one foot and was supposedly a gift from God. Muslims worship this stone, which thousands of years ago fell from the sky."

Chapter 47

Various Locations
Present Time

About the time that Karen's plane took off for New York, all hell broke loose. Saudi news reported that the crash was not an accident. It said that the plane was hijacked, and that the transmission from the plane was "T–3, code 13." All on board, along with an unknown number of people on the ground, were killed instantly.

During the hijacking, there were various reports from passengers speaking on their cell phones. They described gunfire and non-Arabs taking over the plane and more than two-dozen people shot and killed before the crash occurred. The cell phone reports said that the hijackers had brought at least two guns aboard. There was no explanation of how hijackers could get guns through the stringent security check and onto an airplane.

Saudi news reported that the calls were made from the rear of the plane from passengers originally seated further forward in the cabin. This was a sign that passengers and perhaps crew had been moved to the back of the aircraft.

A picture may be worth a thousand words, but a video sound bite is worth a thousand pictures. The uplink satellite feeds from Saudi Arabia quickly sent the story around the world. It was the lead story everywhere. Videos of the aftermath of an attack on the Kaaba showed the smoke still rising.

Many people were killed on the ground. The screeching of ambulance and fire engine sirens and interviews with crying eyewitnesses completed the story. The world media sensed the importance of this story would be similar to what occurred on 9-11. The big questions were who did it and why anyone would want to attack Islam's most important and holy mosque.

One television reporter remarked that in June of 2003, Saudi police fought with enemies of the Royal Saudi family in a foiled plot to attack Mecca, Islam's holiest city. He speculated that this might have been a hijacking gone bad by the same group. Presumably, this was a plot to force the Royal Family from power.

Another reporter said that there were reports of infidels and non-Arabs who committed the hijacking, therefore another explanation was more likely.

Somewhere people laughed and somewhere music played, but not in the land of Islam. Muslims were beside themselves. They believe that the attack upon this building is an affront against God.

An attack on Mecca is strictly forbidden! This is not permitted! It is an act of terror against Allah himself. That this location was attacked is beyond logic. It is beyond belief! It is the most sacrilegious act possible. Nothing can describe it. It is beyond thought. The demonstrations grew and oil prices skyrocketed.

Some mourned, some cried, some attacked anyone who appeared to be a non-Arab. The Middle East was afire with emotions, and the price of oil quickly moved even higher. It was the lead news story everywhere. There was talk of another oil boycott against the west. There were beheadings of unfortunates who were in the wrong place at the wrong time.

The reaction was even larger than Karen thought possible. She knew there would be waves of violence and escalating oil prices, but the level of violence and the extreme of oil prices was a surprise. The following newspaper clippings give a feeling for the Muslim reaction.

Chapter 48

Newspaper Reports
Present Time

The New York Evening Herald reports:

Riots, Violence and Record Oil Prices

Islam found itself caught up in a wave of violent disturbances that swept with a fury through streets and neighborhoods. In some cases, violence occurred spontaneously. In other cases, the violence was organized by Muslim fundamentalists.

There were brutal acts of killing and torture by Arabs. In Jordan, small non-Muslim children were tortured by their murderers before being beheaded. The riots were accompanied by militant Arab slogans such as "Allah is our God and the infidels are dogs." The danger now appears to threaten the very survival of some Arab governments. Many areas still remain under curfew.

Some reports said over one thousand people were killed in the Mecca attack.

Al-Jazeera, the Arab news organization had reported that the Arab League spokesman Hossam Zaki said that the report was wrong and the actual number was closer to three hundred people. Al-Jazeera said that it was not fair for some terrorists to attack innocent people and holy sites. Al-Jazeera went on to report that there are indications that the Mecca attackers didn't plan on getting away. They were probably suicide terrorists who will spend eternity in hell for taking the lives of innocent Muslims.

In Cairo, police opened fire on a rampaging mob, which set ablaze houses and shops and killed 65 persons in the central business district prompting authorities to impose curfews late Saturday night.

People are seething with anger; the pictures of Mecca are everywhere. Every newspaper you pick up in an Arab country has pictures of it. It's like a nightmare that has come to life. One Muslim carried a sign that said, "Every day that infidels take a breath anywhere on this earth is an insult to the Prophet."

Violence broke out in Baghdad Saturday night. Police opened fire and lobbed tear gas shells in the city's Adhamiya neighborhood of northern Baghdad. There, a mob hurling petrol bombs and shooting rocket-propelled grenades killed 39 people.

In Gaza, a fifteen-year-old teenage girl was duped into blowing herself up in Israel, killing twenty-six innocent school children. Thousands of supporters of Hamas celebrated in the streets, and the Associated Press reported that the bomber's mother hailed the attack as "heroic" and said her daughter's soul was "Happy in heaven."

Earlier Saturday, a curfew was announced in Damascus after communal violence broke out in which 26 people were killed and many more injured.

The official death toll of the violence has gone over 858 people since the riots erupted in the wake of the airplane terrorism incident at Mecca two days ago.

Prominent members of the Islamic establishment have called for an immediate end to the riots, violence, looting, and beheadings. Middle East political leaders say that the western countries are cooperating fully in the investigation of what happened in Mecca. They say that the Islamic penalty for attacking Allah's own house is very harsh. It is a deliberate offense against God Himself, and requires the most painful type of death.

Describing the Mecca attack as "a crime against humanity and not against one community," the prime minister of France said that he would support an international investigation to the hilt, and that no stone should be left unturned until the culprit or culprits are found and punished.

From the White House, the President of the United States today expressed his sorrow at the loss of innocent life. He pledges full cooperation with the Saudi Arabian and the French governments in tracking down the perpetrators of the Mecca attack.

At the Vatican, the Pope expressed deep sorrow for the deaths in the attack last week on a mosque in Mecca. He has appealed to followers of all religions to work together for peace and justice.

Oil prices hit another new high as supply fears settled in. On the New York Mercantile Exchange, traders drove up the price of crude futures by almost 35% over yesterday's price. Fears of a probable reduction in supply from Arab countries fueled the rise. The current price of crude oil is now at an all time high. This extreme price is sending shock waves through the industrialized world. The crisis creates great concern on Wall Street, and the Dow Jones Industrial Stock Price Index tumbled.

Chapter 49

Various Locations
Present Time

The e-mails were finally read at the news and broadcast networks and because of the earlier e-mail, and because the message started with "T–3, code 13," much of the media determined that this was an authentic recording.

NBC was the first network to break the story. The e-mails, and attached audio files, were in perfect Parisian French. Karen thought that if the operation can be blamed on the French, so much the better to throw the police off the scent. The entire translated file was read on a special Mecca newscast.

"Greetings from our secret location in France. The name of our group is *T–3*. We are terrorists who terrorize the terrorists, and we take full and sole credit for the attack on Mecca. We are not associated with any government, but are a group of multi-national freedom fighters.

"Muslim terrorists attacked the wrong people. We have had our fill of it, and we are not going to take it anymore. The governments of the world are afraid to respond. We do not fear Islam, and as free people we can respond where governments can not."

"Muslim terrorists are instruments of the Devil. In Islam we see only killing, assassination, conspiracy, kidnapping, beheading and various other bloody gore. I ask you, does that sound like God or the Devil? Muslims are agents of the Anti-Christ, and the predictions said that they would come. We welcome them as a predictor of His second coming.

"We quote from their Koran, the Muslim unholy bible, which proves that they have the devil working within them. Islam is totalitarian and ideas of individualism, freedom, human rights, democracy, or freedom of religion, are unknown to it:

Koran quote 9:5 "Then fight and slay the Infidels wherever you find them, seize them, beleaguer them, and lie in wait for them in every stratagem of war."

Koran quote 9:73 "Make war on the Infidels and hypocrites and deal rigorously with them."

Koran quote 8:39 "Make war on the Infidels until idolatry shall cease and God's religion shall reign supreme."

Koran quote 4:89 "Seize the Infidels and slay them wherever you find them: and in any case take no friends or helpers from their ranks."

"Can you believe these are actual quotes from the Koran, their so-called bible? Islam is not a religion, it is an unholy political cult that has decided to kill people who have real religions.

"Asymmetric war techniques are the practice of attacking a more powerful enemy's weak spots. But when civilians are targeted instead of military targets, it is called terrorism. Many terrorists are more than happy to target innocent civilians in their cause of spreading Islam throughout the world. Our answer is to take a page from them and attack Islam itself, instead of trying to find small individual terrorist groups. They must understand that there are consequences to their actions. Their most revered cities and symbols will be destroyed. They have underestimated our anger and resolve for justice.

"The city of Mecca is a natural place to begin the attack. Mecca is the home base of terror. It is the capital of what should really be called *The United Islamic Republic*. We have brought your terror home to roost. Only Muslims are allowed into Mecca so we can be assured that no free men will be accidentally injured. The message we want to send is that the mosques in Mecca are equivalent to our trade centers and schools. You think your terrorists are bad guys? Well, we are one hundred times as bad.

"Terrorists think they have found our weakness. They think they can kill our civilians, and we will only try to attack the elusive fighters hiding in caves and holes in the ground. They know that we cannot defend ourselves against an unseen enemy. They mistake our kindness and compassion for weakness. They do not understand our real strength. They do not understand that our freedom is much stronger that their sixth century superstition.

"Islamic terrorists thought that they were strong and we were weak. But Islamic terror is not strong. We have found your weakness. This weakness is your many holy sacred sites. For us, life is more sacred than sites. If your terrorists take our lives, we will take your sites. 'Tit for tat' is our motto, and your sacred sites are the targets. If people are killed at these holy sites, too bad. Remember war is hell and you started it.

"Allah does not want you to force us to destroy Mecca and similar sights of importance to Islam. If you don't stop attacking our civilians you will take the full responsibility for the destruction of these sites. You must be proactive and find those who would commit terror and turn them in to the authorities. You must stop preaching hatred of non-Muslims. You must treat us as you would want to be treated.

"You will not think, till you are compelled to think. When you find yourselves face to face with a greater and more enduring strength than your own, you will renounce their terror.

"But you need solid proof that terror doesn't work. You cannot be driven from their positions by a little paper shot. Killing a few terrorists is not a solution. In your present mood, if you hear an appeal to pity, sensibility, and sympathy, you take it for a cry of weakness. But an attack on Mecca will give you an opportunity to review your position.

"We've demonstrated our willingness to attack you at your most valued targets. It was not our intention to cause great loss of life or completely destroy the city in the first attack. The attack did not occur during the Hajj season. This first attack was only a warning. If the terrorists do not heed our warning, then we will attack again. We will continue to destroy your most important targets as long as you continue terrorizing free people.

"We have the weapons and delivery systems to attack any time we choose. Mecca will be turned into a radioactive wasteland for hundreds of years. No pilgrimages to Mecca will be possible to those who condone terror. We may also target other sites such as Muhammad's tomb in Medina.

"It's a fiction that you do not have a home address where we can retaliate. We have found your address. We know your address. It is Ground 0 Mecca.

"Every time we defend ourselves by blowing up your important sites, we want to mention the names of your religious leaders who brought this upon you. Today the names of those responsible are Osama Bin Laden, Muqtada Al-Sadr, Shamil Basayev and Anas Kamal Mostafa. The next time we attack your headquarters, we will again give you the names of the men responsible for that attack. You must control your terrorists if you want Islam to survive.

"We ask those Muslims who want peace, and who want to keep their holy sites, to infiltrate these groups and identify the terrorist killers. Turn in the terrorists and tell the authorities of their plans. It is important since only you can save Islam's holy sites.

"The world is at war with the terrorists. We are joining the war on the side of freedom. The whole world is our battlefield, and every radical Muslim is an enemy soldier.

General Pierre Beauregard
Nuclear Battle Group
T-3"

Chapter 50

Various Locations
Present Time

The Holy Black Stone (the Hajr-al-aswad) is enclosed in a silver ring. Some say the stone came from God and fell from heaven, but it is probably a meteorite. Muslims worship this large black stone. On their required pilgrimage to Mecca, many faithful seek the blessing of the black stone and touch, or even actually kiss, this stone as if it were an idol of some God. It is displayed in the eastern corner of the Kaaba.

The airplane hit from the west side of the Kaaba. Since it is a big building and absorbed the blast fairly well, the black stone escaped destruction. Even if the stone was on the west side, it's terribly hard to destroy a meteorite that already hit the earth at thousands of miles per hour. The outer cover of a meteorite is called a fusion crust. It's the result of extreme heating as the meteorite falls to earth through our atmosphere. You could almost say the meteorite was beyond destruction, because it was already destroyed during its landing on earth.

One prominent Islamic leader said, "It is a miracle! The Kaaba was almost totally destroyed but the Hajr-al-aswad, this gift from God, was unscathed. It is proof of the power of Allah and his prophet Muhammad! There is no God but Allah, and Muhammad is His messenger."

Other Islamic leaders proclaimed that the Kaaba would be quickly rebuilt, as it has many times in the past, and the stone would be put back in its rightful place as if nothing had happened. This miracle helped quiet the Muslims and the riots in Islamic cities begin to subside.

The Arab leaders continued to speak of the miracle and the need to end the riots and to get back to normal life. They also demanded a United Nations investigation into the French involvement in the attack. They insisted that this infidel terrorist group be hunted down and executed. By the end of the next day, calm was established in all major countries.

The thought of possible large-scale damage to Mecca was more than the Islamic leaders could stand. Most of the leaders stopped making their jihad and "kill the infidel" speeches. Many leaders asked for those with knowledge of terrorist plots to report it to the authorities.

The war to establish Islam as the law of the world went through various stages during the last 1400 years. Sometimes it was a hot war with rapid territory expansion. Sometimes it was a cold war and a time to consolidate their gains. The raid on Mecca put the Islamic war against the infidels on the back burner to cool off. Things could not be allowed to continue along the current path. Mecca could not be destroyed. A better way of defeating the infidels would have to be discovered.

Human nature has always made available the capacity for vicious and brutal behavior. Left unchecked, most of us have the nature to accept, or even be entertained by, violence and death. Society can either encourage or prohibit this behavior. It's no surprise that a doctrine such as Islam can encourage this brutal behavior. Because they now recognize the consequences of their holy war, Islamic leaders have decided to temporally make this behavior unacceptable.

Some Muslim terrorist leaders were rounded up and jailed on various charges. Funding for the paramilitary groups began to dry up.

There was a marked decrease in suicide bombers. Intelligence begins to come in from Muslim sources affecting the apprehension of terrorists. The T-3 war on terror was working.

Chapter 51

News Reports
Present Time

The AP wire service reports:
Put More Air Marshals on Airplanes

Saudi authorities are not sure how the Mecca hijackers smuggled their guns on board, but they promise they will intensify airport screening. Starting Monday they will require passengers to remove their coats during the screening. It is thought that a gun, or guns, made of non-metallic, high-tech plastic material was used by the hijackers. Reports from a number of passengers using their cell phones confirm that the hijackers had guns, and that there was a gunfight between them and the passengers.

It is not known how many hijackers there were, but if they had guns, only a small number would have been needed. Saudi authorities said that 100% of all flights would now have armed air marshals. Screeners will also be given greater authority to pat down and search passengers to be sure they do not have the plastic guns. Additional equipment to scan for traces of explosives will also be installed.

Critics say the additional measures will make some people, especially Muslim women, feel uncomfortable. A frequent flier to Saudi Arabia, Jon Malone, an oil field engineer who represents Texas Drilling and Tool, calls the changes "a farce." Mr. Malone said that he doubts the new searches will improve security. He said that anyone could easily get around the new screening if they wanted to. He went on to say that it is possible that the guns were planted by people who work for the Saudi Airlines or for the Athens Eleftherios Venizelos International Airport.

Other passengers disagree. "It's a no-brainer," said Muhammad Yusuf Abdullah, a Saudi citizen. "Given a choice, I would want more security rather than less."

The AP wire service reports:
One Hijacker identified

Monday the Paris Reporter said police were hunting for a man living in Paris for his part in connection with Mecca hijacking. A spokesperson for the French secret service said, "We are not denying the report, but there is no charge against him. He is just a person of interest wanted strictly for questioning."

The Paris Reporter identified the possible Mecca hijacker as a French citizen with a French passport. He was referred to the French secret service by a cell phone message from one of the passengers as a very tall and large man with gray hair. Airport security cameras have a picture of this hijacker, and his picture led to his identification. He is a Frenchman and his name is Maurice J. Duvall. He left the Athens airport with a French passport. However, at this time, very little else is known about him. This information puts France on the defensive; they are trying to get more information about Mr. Duvall.

The AP wire service reports:

Mecca Hijacking Reaction

Mohamed Ali Aden, who commanded 350 men in the recent war, said he would settle for nothing less than a full-fledged Islamic state.

"If you will not join Islam, you are not my brother," he said. "I am a holy warrior and those who disturb Islam, we will disturb them.

"We've neglected God's verses for so long," Mr. Aden said in an interview. "We want our women veiled and we want them at home. We men have to grow our beards."

The AP wire service reports:

A source close to France's anti-terrorism service, speaking on condition of anonymity, spoke of the similarities between Tuesday's bombings and earlier attacks on his government's headquarters and a police station.

"See how your children and neighbors are uniting against the banner of jihad and against its mistaken leaders," he said. "I call for the overthrow of the leaders of the radical Muslims and their support for the war of terror against innocent civilians."

The AP wire service reports:

Mecca Hijacking Investigation

French officials on Tuesday said that the investigation could take weeks or possibly months. They cautioned that the identity of this one hijacker does not prove that all the hijackers were French or that this was a French plot, but the new revelations, coupled with the fact that the communication from the "T–3" group was e-mailed from France, became a definite embarrassment to the French nation that bills itself as a friend of many Arab states. The political ramifications of the attack could poison French and Arab relations.

An unidentified source said that authorities were tipped off that a French group in Paris might be involved in the hijacking. The source also said that this small group of middle-aged men that called themselves the Cojecks, has been under investigation for almost two years. None of the members were Muslims. During a raid yesterday, this group was found in possession of knives, hundreds of dollars of money and a book titled *Why I Am Not a Muslim*. This book is very critical of Islam. One member of this hate group works at the Charles de Gaulle Airport. He may have contributed to smuggling guns on board an airplane going from Paris to Athens where they were transferred to the hijacked aircraft.

The AP wire service reports:

Louvre Terror Attack

Today, a fundamentalist Muslim terrorist set off an explosion that destroyed part of the Louvre Art Museum in Paris. The explosion was centered in the Boucher Room and the resulting smoke and fire damaged surrounding areas.

Orange flames and thick smoke occurred when the terrorist poured petrol from a fake stomach pouch on the floor of the Boucher Room. A timer fuse ignited it a few minutes later and the gas exploded resulting in a firestorm. A number of people were injured. The exact number and the extent of their injuries is not known at this time.

The fundamentalist Muslim terrorist fled the scene but was caught two blocks from the Louvre. He quickly admitted to the allegation of setting the petrol bomb and said he did it in repayment for French complicity in the Mecca attack. He also said he attacked the art because paintings of people and animals are not allowed under Islamic law. The alleged terrorist, whose name was withheld in accordance with lawful practices of the assumption of innocence and for confidentiality, said, "Everyone should be more respectful of Islamic laws. All pictures of animals and people should be immediately removed from their walls."

Islamic scholars say that in Muhammad's day there was still idol worship, so Muhammad cursed the painters of men and animals. Consequently drawings of people and animals were not allowed. Islam still prohibits this type of art depicting people or animals to prevent worship of false idols. Islamic art does not include people and is instead mostly landscaped designs and patterns.

The Musée du Louvre said that many irreplaceable paintings were destroyed, but the museum would, hopefully, be open in the next few months, with just a dozen or fewer rooms remaining closed.

Chapter 52

News Reports
Present Time

The New York Evening Herald reports:
Hijacker's Mistaken Identity

One of the Mecca hijackers who is identified as a French citizen by the name of Maurice J. Duvall is still alive and living in Paris. Mr. Duvall said that he was on a cruise ship last year when his passport disappeared. He gave his passport to a cruise line official as required by the cruise line, but he never got it back. The missing passport was reported to the French embassy shortly after it was discovered missing.

Authorities are investigating the connection between the missing passport and the hijacker who used Mr. Duvall's name. The passport number on the hijacker's passport could not have been the same as on Mr. Duvall's passport. If the number was the same, it would have triggered an alert, however no alert was recorded. So far, there are no clues except for the surveillance camera photograph. The photograph of the suspect has been widely circulated in the hope that someone will recognize it.

The New York Evening Herald reports:
The New Enemy of Terrorism is Terrorism

A usually reliable source in the White House reports that the President is not happy with the terrorist attack in Mecca and believes that it is not the way things should be done. He said that America would do everything in its power to assist France and Saudi Arabia to catch the terrorists. However, the President went on to repeat an old quote that says a man who lives by the sword should die by the sword.

The New York Evening Herald Editorial by Greg Odoms:

Islam Should be Closed Down

There were public reports from our secret service that recruitment for the Islamic jihad still continues in many mosques. If the mosques teach that Muslims should kill infidels, then they do not teach religion. God does not teach killing. The Devil teaches killing and then deflowering seventy-two virgins.

If in a mosque there is recruitment for Islamic jihad, it is not a house of God. It is a house of war. If it's a house of war seeking to overthrow our free government, it should be closed down.

A cruel justice was served in the use of an airplane against the Islamic command center. The Islamic terrorist animals, cloaked in human disguise, have been revenged by an idea that had its origins in their own perverted Islamic thinking.

The New York Evening Herald reports:

Saudi Flight SV212 had an Air Marshal

The latest report from Saudi Arabian Airlines flight SV212 indicated that the hijacked Mecca flight had an air marshal on board. They said he was probably identified by the hijackers and then shot before he could fight back. The airline refused to disclose what percentage of their flights have air marshals. They also would not respond to a question concerning placing more than one air marshal on a flight.

Chapter 53

Chicago
Present Time

Karen flew to Chicago to meet with Saleh, the spokesperson for the secret group that planned the Mecca attack. Saleh had his office in Chicago. It had everything he needed from a big city, but it was not a city where a spy would normally live. New York and Washington - now they were spy cities, but mid-west Chicago was considered just an industrial center.

Saleh did not want Karen to know where his office was located so they needed to meet in a neutral place rented for the day. A meeting room is preferable to a regular hotel room because it would be unexpected, and being unpredictable is what his business was all about. It would have been safer to communicate only by secure e-mail. Still, they had to have this face-to-face meeting to review the Mecca attack and talk about future operations.

Karen and Saleh arrived separately at the Fairmont Chicago Hotel in downtown Chicago. It was an unlikely setting to hold a meeting of such importance, but it was private and safe.

Saleh had reserved the hotel's smallest meeting facilities for their meeting. The taxicab dropped Saleh off a few blocks away and he walked to the hotel. Saleh came down Columbus Drive and arrived about an hour before Karen. At the hotel, Saleh routinely swept the room for listening devices and found it clean.

Karen arrived later dressed in a conservative blue pinstriped business suit that exuded a dignified businesswoman aura. This is not Karen's favorite dress, but long ago she learned that people put an illogical amount of credence in how one dresses. The clothes you wear can get you noticed, or help you blend in. In Karen's business you want to be an invisible person.

After their unbelievably spectacular success, one couldn't be too careful. A surveillance camera at the airport probably had pictures of all people going through security screening. These pictures did incorrectly identify Major Sevorov after a description of him was cell phoned from one of the passengers on the plane. French agents were even now desperately trying to correctly identify Major Sevorov. They surely asked the security agencies of most countries for help in the identification. Still, there is not much incentive for Russia to help identify Major Sevorov, since it would just switch the Arab anger from France to Russia. Most likely, the Russian intelligence people would go through the motions, but not volunteer any useful information. Nevertheless, Karen assumed that Major Sevorov would sooner or later be identified.

Even if, or when, Major Sevorov is identified, there would be no real link between him and Karen. All their communications were done with the most elaborate security. The payments were wire transfers and arranged in such a way that there was no money trail. They were never seen in public. Still, Sevorov may have told someone something, or left some clue.

Craig would be almost impossible to identify. His body and face changed so much since his illness began that even his friends would have had to look twice to recognize him. His picture was probably taken by the airport security cameras, but he was such a non-descript person that the odds of a positive identification were infinitesimal.

Karen went through the Athens' security screening an hour before the Russian. They might wonder why she arrived so early for her plane, but that would be it. Karen's picture was certainly in various files but she wore a hat that shielded most of her face from the camera. However, there was still the possibility that some camera could have taken a picture that was good enough to match up with her.

Karen certainly had a working cover story for her trip to Athens, and there were thousands of people leaving the Athens airport that day, but the possibilities are endless. It just means that from now on, everyone had to be extra cautious at all times.

Chapter 54

Chicago
Present Time

When Karen arrived at the Fairmont Chicago Hotel meeting room, Saleh jumped up and hugged her. He felt like celebrating. "You did just great," he said with a big satisfied smile on his face. "Everything worked out perfectly."

"Saleh, I am surprised that you decided on a face-to-face meeting with me instead of an e-mail."

Saleh gave a gentle laugh. "Karen, one does not say goodbye to such a successful operation with an e-mail or a fax."

Karen smiled and asked, "How did you know that the Muslim violence would subside and not just grow and grow?"

"There was a possibility that Muslim fundamentalists would go crazy and declare full-scale conventional war on free people, but this would also be good. In that type of war, they would be defeated in short order. Still, this is only a lull in the terror, and the war will begin again. Radical Islam still is at war with the west, and yet many people don't even want to acknowledge that there is a problem!

"The terrorists' only real power is that freedom-loving countries will not really fight back. Somehow freedom-loving countries believe that they should follow the Geneva Convention, even though these feudal fanatical Muslim terrorists never gave any thought to following it.

"And that is what happens with the news media still sticking their heads in the sand believing that the radical Muslims are just God-fearing people. In fact, the news media is still stumbling along and reminds me of the clown car at the circus. You know the cars with the unbalanced frame, partially breaking up along with multiple loud explosions, but somehow it just keep going along while everyone laughs?

"There may be a lot of innocent people killed. Collateral damage it's called, but freedom demands constant vigilance. To give your life for freedom is an honor and a requirement for the advancement of mankind.

"Karen, I must congratulate you on this mission. That was a brilliant idea, creating that French cover story for the Russians, and blaming the French for the attack. I think we rattled the terrorists' cage pretty hard," said Saleh after they sat down at the conference table.

"I read their play book. The *Al Qaeda Terrorism Manual* suggested spreading rumors and writing statements that instigate people against the enemy. France has not been helpful against terrorism. I thought that figuratively planting the French flag in the operation seemed the thing to do to throw suspicion away from us.

"It was poetic. Everything went even better than planned. We accomplished all three of our goals. The terrorists now realize that countries and boarders do not fool us and that we know who they are and that their headquarters is located in Mecca. The terrorists now know that we can, and will, seek revenge for their attacks. Free people everywhere now realize that the terrorists' aim is global domination. They know that this domination message is approved, and even encouraged, by the mosques. The mosques repeat the holy war messages until some weak-minded people physically act out their parts."

Karen was awed by the praise and by what a sophisticated and efficient covert organization she had created. She looked up at Saleh with clear, slightly humorous eyes and asked, "I just don't understand it. Why do these evil people want to kill us?"

"They want to save you!"

"Huh?"

"Yes. Muslims say that you pray to Jesus instead of praying to Allah. There is only one God and Allah is his name. Any other belief is false, like praying to idols. The concept of praying to a son of Allah is beyond belief."

"Oh, God! Do you feel that way?"

"I do! But I, and most Muslims, would not use force to convert you to the truth. In a free world you are allowed to go to hell, if you don't believe."

"Wow! That is totally weird. But as long as you are on the side of free choice, I suppose I support you."

"Our individual beliefs have nothing to do with our respect for the beliefs of others. That's what we are fighting, a mistaken philosophy of 'believe in my way or die.'

"But I do feel bad about all the innocent people who died as a result of our victory. How do you handle it?"

"I don't feel anything about it. I don't have a problem with killing and never have."

"That makes you seem like a sociopath or something."

"Don't be silly. The definition of a sociopath has to do with an extreme antisocial behavior and a total lack of conscience. That does not describe me. I have no feelings about killing people, because I accept that we will all die, and in comparison to the sixteen billion year life of our universe, we will all die in the blink of an eye. I think I am one of the few sane people who can make the hard decisions of life and death in unique situations.

"Remember this: The goal of the radicals is not to win every battle. Their goal is, through propaganda and actions, to appear like winners and thus build an army of believers who will eventually take over the world. If moderate Muslims realize that the terrorist violence is not working, they will stop condoning that behavior and it won't be long before the terror will stop.

"But enough of that. Let's move on to the next subject, and I have some great news! We made 377 million dollars because of our attack!"

"Oh, my God," she exclaimed, and almost fainted. "You said million didn't you?" She knew they would do well, but 377 million. "Did you sell that many oil futures contracts?"

"Yes. We only bet on sure things. Demand for oil is very inflexible, and the world has so little spare production capacity that perceived disruptions of production can raise prices dramatically. After the attack the price of oil rose very high. You don't have to be a rocket scientist to know that when the Muslim terrorists have the equivalent of a 9-11 happen to them, there can be disruptions and oil prices will spike up. Knowing this would happen we bought thousands of oil futures options. We bought them through overseas numbered accounts so they would be more difficult to track.

"In oil futures options, there is tremendous leverage. A few dollars could easily make thousands of dollars profit, and it did. After the value went up, we quickly sold. We knew that the oil contracts were bound to come down from these over-exaggerated highs. It made us a bundle"

Saleh's group bought oil futures contracts a few days before the jet crashed into the Kaaba. Each oil futures contract controls 1,000 barrels (42,000 gallons) of crude oil. They are highly leveraged so that a relatively small investment can bring huge returns. These oil contracts are very popular instruments. They are bought and sold all the time. Often people buy contracts and sell them the next day or even the next hour. Knowing in advance when oil prices are going up or down works wonders.

This was a sure thing. Saleh and his group knew that every time there is serious political unrest in the Middle East, oil prices go up. Therefore, they knew that oil prices would rise after the Kaaba attack. They thought the price would go up five dollars a barrel, but the price actually shot up much more. Their gain exceeded their greatest expectations.

"I'm sorry for being dense, but I want to be sure I heard right. Did you say that you made 377 million for crashing one airplane?"

"Yes, and we will do even better next time. But I want to be sure that you understand that you should not get involved with oil futures. You would be an outsider and stick out like a sore thumb. T-3 has professionals who trade large oil contracts regularly. They create no suspicions."

"What are you going to do with all that money?"

"First we have to pay all the expenses that we already incurred from the Mecca attack. That includes the agreed payment to you, which was deposited this morning in your Cayman Islands account. We also paid Craig's family and the Russians."

"Of course there is a whole lot of money left over. Our motivation is to amass a war chest of money. We need it to fund bigger and better future raids against terrorist targets. With all this money, and our natural love of freedom, we cannot fail. Money will buy power that can be focused against terrorists."

"This first attack was not revenge but a warning. We purposely choose the timing so that it would not be during their month of Ramadan when they make their hajj to the Mecca pilgrimage sites, but we don't want them to know that we tried to minimize loss of life. We want the terrorists to believe that we are vicious and will stop at nothing. We want them to believe that we have targeted their headquarters and that we mean business.

"Western governments somehow believe that a rigorous defense will defeat terrorism. Nothing can be further from the truth. Prior to the Second World War, France built the Maginot Line to defend themselves against Germany. It was a total failure. Defense never wins. Defense cannot permanently keep the enemy from scoring. Eventually, they are bound to score.

"We are not part of any government whose hands are tied by rules and by bureaucrats. We are completely independent and can do whatever works. We are a secret organization, and we can't be found. Our offensive against the source of radical Islamic terror is something that governments are not willing to do.

"Now, radical Muslims will know terror as they have never known it before. It is not just their lives that are at risk. It is the very symbols of their way of life. These are the symbols that condone terror against civilians.

"Some people in our group thought the solution to answer the 9-11 Muslim terrorist attacks was a high-tech strike, but the low-tech option seemed more fitting. We decided on low-tech against their most valuable target. We thought that this would scare them, and it did. It makes our high-tech capabilities all the more respectable.

"The terrorists assume that they can't be retaliated against. For example, Russia's defense minister, Sergei B. Ivanov, speaking in Moscow after all those school children were murdered said, "War has been declared on us, where the enemy is unseen and there is no front." We disagree. It is irrational to make a distinction between the radical Muslim leaders and the militias who do the terrorizing. These militants receive their "holy war" training and instructions from these Muslim leaders.

"The front is the institutions that promote terrorism. The front is the mosques that preach political terror. This is the enemy that we will attack.

"We now have enough money to plan and launch a number of attacks on their headquarters. We also have enough to buy a few nuclear weapons and also some delivery systems. Most people do not know that Soviet military forces deployed about 22,000 small tactical nuclear warheads. They did not have individual identification numbers and some are no longer in Russian government control. With the current situation in Russia, we are able to find the right people who control some of these warheads. For the right price and the right cause, they are available.

"We can get a Russian plutonium fission nuclear bomb for twenty-six million dollars. It's plenty big enough to wipe out most of Qom and poison the ground and turn it into a radioactive waste heap for hundreds of years. The Russians hate the radical Muslim terrorists, so they are quite willing to look the other way for that amount of money. And after Mecca, the Russian mafia will trust us enough to sell us the bomb."

"But two of their men died in that crash. Won't they be angry?"

"No. Sevorov was a real pain for the mafia. They knew that it would probably be terminal, so no problem."

"Saleh. What is this Qom? It would be far better to attack the high profile terrorist leaders in places like the western Pakistan boarder area."

"Those leaders are more valuable to us alive as a symbol of Hitler-like evil. To kill these infamous people would only make them martyrs and a new set of leaders would take their place. No, we are going after the very source of evil"

"I am beginning to see. It makes sense, but tell me more about this Qom."

"Qom is a city in Iran almost 100 miles south-west of Tehran. It is an important holy city for Shi'a Muslims. The city is the largest center for Shi'a radical Muslim scholarship in the world, and is best known for its radical Islam University, Howzeh-ye Elmieh. It attracts a lot of students from all over the world who want to become radical mullahs. Ayatollah Khomeini, the radical who disposed the moderate Shaw of Iran, is probably the most famous among those who studied there."

Karen had a thoughtful expression on her face and said, "After all this, I imagine that the radical Muslims terrorists will have to sign a peace treaty with us anti-terrorists."

"That may happen, but it's not likely."

"Well then, what's the answer?" asked Karen.

"With communism, the peace was kept out of fear of the reprisal. They called it MAD, which is an acronym for mutually assured destruction. I guess it will eventually be the same with the radical Muslims. Our goal is just to reverse the trend of power gains by this radical faction."

"Now that I am a full member of T-3, can you tell me more about the group?"

"I really do not know a whole lot, but they were the force working behind the scenes in the Mecca campaign. They made sure the entry visas were authentic and the passports would be honored. They made sure only one air marshal was on that airplane and probably did a lot more that we do not know about."

"How did they do it?"

"I don't know, but they do have connections, and that is all I can say."

"OK. On to a new subject. Dr. Jackson wants me to ask you if your group would consider eliminating the family members of some of the 9-11 terrorists. He said a car bomb or something of that nature at the homes of the parents and brothers would give him more closure. He would be happy to pay for part of it."

Saleh shook his head, "No, we are more into the big picture. There is no doubt that young terrorists might think twice about terror if they knew their families would face the consequences of their actions. However, that is for someone else to do. We are not interested in those poor souls who were duped into committing violence. We are interested in their top leaders who promote and sponsor it. We are interested in targets of particular symbolic value. We will specialize in going after terrorist learning centers and holy sites that are the very center of terror. A bomb at a terror school has a much higher physiological significance than just killing some family."

"He will be disappointed to hear that."

"We don't want you to even answer his request. We want you to break off all contact with Dr. Jackson. The airport cameras probably have pictures of everyone who went through security. Because of the fake passports, it will be difficult to tie a picture in with the flight that crashed, but they have their ways. It is possible that Craig's real identity will somehow be discovered. If that happens, everyone he knew will be contacted. Keep away from Dr. Jackson.

"Sevorov or Nick might eventually be identified, and there is always a slight possibility that it could point to you. Even though you took maximum precautions to keep your identity secret, you may yet become a person of interest. We have to assume the worst, so be sure to remove all traces of your past communications. Please destroy your computer hard drive. Don't just erase it because the information can still be recovered. After you erase it, remove the drive and beat it hard with a hammer until it is destroyed. This will make it impossible for anyone to recover the data. Then throw the drive in some business's dumpster. Leave nothing to chance. Get rid of anything that might suggest that you had a part in this mission."

"That's already done. What do you think the Muslim fundamentalists' answer will be?"

"They are doing the devil's work, and there is no telling what the devil will have them do next. Now that we have the money, we can move ahead with plans for the Qom strike. God is on our side and has provided the sustenance for our continuing mission. We will be ready for them.

"The only solution is for the radical terrorists to understand that we see them for who they really are. They need to know that we are many times stronger than they are and we are not afraid to attack their vulnerable targets. Civilized governments are afraid to attack terrorist headquarters, but we have no restrictions. The balance of power has shifted. They will soon come to understand this truth.

"They say that it isn't over until the fat lady sings. She is singing now! If they don't hear it yet, they will soon be overwhelmed by the song."

Chapter 55

Chicago
Present Time

A Tomahawk cruise missile is basically a small, pilot less airplane. The Tomahawk Block IV cruise missile is 20 feet long and 21 inches in diameter. It is so small that it has a very small electronic cross-section and is very effective at evading detection by enemy radar.

After launch from a tube only slightly bigger than the missile, the wings, tail fins, and air inlet unfold. The wingspan is 8.5 feet and the missile has a cruising speed of 550 mph.

There are new cruise designs that fly to the target at speeds of over 4,000 miles per hour, much faster than the Tomahawk, but anything faster that 769 mph at sea level (less at higher altitudes) trails a sonic boom, and the loud noise is a dead giveaway that something is coming. By contrast, the Tomahawk is relatively quite and stealthy.

The Tomahawk is powered by turbofan jet engines and can fly to targets at 500 to 1,553 miles depending on the configuration. Its job in life is to deliver up to a 1,000-pound bomb to its target. It can also deliver a thermonuclear bomb. As you would guess, the missile is entirely and completely destroyed beyond recognition when the thermonuclear bomb explodes.

Once launched, the missile cruises to its target on its inertial guidance system in conjunction with terrain contour matching and its global positioning satellite (GPS) systems. The GPS system uses the GPS satellites and an onboard GPS receiver to detect its position with extremely high accuracy. It is said that the Tomahawk can fly 1000 miles and hit a target the size of an automobile. The Tomahawk is manufactured by Raytheon Missile Systems located in Tucson, Arizona.

Two years ago, sixty-three-year-old Commander Ronald Miles retired from the Navy with full benefits. He thought he would have a full life and looked forward to traveling with his wife, however his wife died last year and he is now bored and looking for something to do with his time. He was an engineer and an expert in the use of Tomahawk cruise missiles and modern weapons. For the last thirteen years, he worked with the United States Navel Armament Research Development Center, and Tucson-based Raytheon Missile Systems. This is exactly the kind of person Karen needs for her next assignment.

Chapter 56

Chicago
Present Time

Commander Ronald Miles and Karen arranged to meet at Buckingham Fountain in Grant Park near downtown Chicago. Karen liked initial meetings in public places, but still private enough where they could not be overheard. Karen wore a bright red scarf so that Commander Miles would recognize her. He saw her, smiled, and walked over.

"Commander Miles?" Karen asked. She recognized him from his picture in her file. He wore a moustache and thick horn-rimmed glasses and was tall but stoop shouldered and leaning forward slightly as if his back hurt.

"Ah, Karen," he replied, as he shook her hand. Karen noticed that he spoke softly, smiled easily, and had a Boston accent.

They walked together, making small talk, and Miles stopped a moment to tamp down his tobacco pipe and fire it up, took a few puffs, then continued to walk with a jaunty tilt to his head. Watching him carefully, Karen immediately realized that Miles was an egotistic man who had strong opinions that mattered only to himself. That was the key to his personality that Karen was looking for.

They continued for a few minutes, then sat down on a secluded park bench and Karen continued to study him carefully. She then started to question Commander Miles about his views on fundamentalist Muslim terror.

"As you know, we are in a war against Muslim fundamentalist terror. Most people do not understand what Islam is about. Most people simple say it is a religion like Christianity, but many of those people are dead wrong.

"Islam is a political ideology. It is a political organization that desires to control the world. It is also a cultural ideology that claims to be right and has the audacity to claim that all other cultures are wrong. The goal of Islam is to subjugate the world. Its doctrine is that the church and the state are one and Islam is the only church and the only state."

Commander Miles cleared his throat and ran his hand through his salt-and-pepper hair. "But isn't it just the extreme fanatics who want to take over the world?" he asked.

"Our enemy in the war against Muslim terror is not just a fringe military group like the monsters who make up al-Qaeda. It is the hundreds of millions of people in the Muslim world who condone their actions, and make the terrorists into heroes. They make it acceptable for the radicals to continue to kill."

Commander Miles shrugged his shoulders and said, "I agree with what you are saying about fundamentalist Muslims; however the newspapers and electronic media say that countries like Afghanistan and Iran are the only countries that harbor terrorists."

With a gruff laugh, Karen replied, "Not so! In the free world the prime element of organization is the country. The country is then subdivided into regions, states, nationalities or religions. In Islam they start with the teachings of Muhammad and then subdivide into countries. The teachings of Muhammad, rather than the country they live in, is how Muslims view themselves. Militant Muslims say they are not from any country and proceed to spread terror in various free world countries. Our answer must not be to try to eliminate individual terrorists or groups. This will never work because of those hundreds of millions of Muslims who tacitly approve of terror. New groups will sprout up faster than weeds in a jungle.

"Why do people join those radical Muslim groups to become terrorists and blow themselves up?

"I read a book called *The True Believer* by Eric Hoffer. He did a good job of explaining it. He said that many people like fundamental religion because they do not have to think. The group provides all answers to life. By contrast, freedom to make your own decisions places the whole blame of failure on the shoulders of the individual, and this can be very scary.

"Also, these fanatic people are attracted to the soul-stirring exhilaration and excitement of working for a cause bigger than they are. This has caused active mass movements for thousands of years. If the enthusiasm, fervor and wild hope of the cause can be shattered, people will abandon the cause and new recruits will dry up.

"What can be done to shatter their enthusiasm and abandon their terror?

"The world has rules and if you break them there are consequences. Attacks cause counter attacks. When weak states like the Islamic countries attack a strong people such as the free democratic people of the world, the weak states lose. These are the rules. The destruction in Mecca is just a warning of these rules.

"The war on terror is a different type of war. In other wars we can identify the name of the enemy. But in this war the identity is not some country, but this leader or that leader. But when we capture or kill this leader, two more spring forward to take his place.

"We are in the process of a historic war between the world of western freedom and the radical Islamic world. Hamas, al-Qaeda, and similar organizations seek to impose worldwide Islamic rule. They believe it is their duty to create the conditions for the return of Mahdi, which is the day of the resurrection. These conditions include a clash of civilizations with the west and many global disasters that trigger grief and sorrow.

"The free countries know the truth about the radical Islamic ideology but treat it as if it is only a religion. Somehow it is politically incorrect to name radical Islam as our real enemy. It is as if the rules say that only our radical enemy is allowed to verbalize what is happening."

"How about international rules?"

"The terrorists totally reject western rules and influence. They see terror as the most effective means to overthrow the infidel regimes, spread Islam, and establish Islamic rule. They are, however, prepared to make a pretense of going along with the western democratic rules and exploit them to remove the infidel regimes, propagate Islam, install Islamic rule, and then eliminate democracy.

"That's the reason why we are here. We plan to attack the foundations of Muslim terror instead of attempting to find and punish individual terrorists. Like the radical Muslims, we will not follow the normal rules. This is the only answer to terror. But before I go into details, I want to know if you would be interested in doing something to help defeat terror. We are talking about technical assistance to the forces of freedom. I assure you that the rewards for this job are impressive. The pay is great and it would be only a few months."

"I want you to think about it and meet me tomorrow. But no one must know about this. Phone me tomorrow. If you are still interested, we will talk about more details."

Chapter 57

Chicago
Present Time

Karen's group was able to pay a bankrupt mid-level employee at Raytheon Missile Systems to steal a Tomahawk cruise missile. The tip came from Saleh, who seemed to have an endless source of information.

It was one of the missiles slated for destructive testing, but the report on the test was faked and the Tomahawk was taken. But there was no way they could steal the W-80 thermo-nuclear warhead that had been developed for the Tomahawk. American nuclear weapon security was too good for that feat.

The W-80 is the warhead used on the cruise missile. It is quite small, only 11.9 inches in diameter and 31.5 inches long. It is also very light and weighs about 290 pounds.

But the small size doesn't mean it is not powerful. The W-80 is a variable yield thermonuclear weapon that can be set from 5 kilotons of TNT, at the low end, to 150 kilotons of TNT at the high end. By means of comparison, the nuclear bomb that destroyed Hiroshima, Japan was13.5 kilotons. The one that destroyed Nagasaki was 22 kilotons. They both exploded about 2,000 feet above their targets and destroyed the cities.

The variable yield function of the W-80 is accomplished by injecting an amount of lithium deuteride (a compound of deuterium and tritium gas) into the vacuum of the hollow core inside the fission-type nuclear weapon. The amount of the lithium deuteride gas will determine the yield. This gas creates the fission part of the thermonuclear weapon. This weapon is commonly referred to as a hydrogen bomb because deuterium is an isotope of hydrogen.

For their second meeting Commander Miles and Karen again met at Buckingham Fountain.

"Commander Miles, it's good to see you again," said Karen as she walked up to him and shook his hand. "Let me come right to the point. What did you decide?"

"You said that I would have to travel to another country, but that I would only be a technical person, and would be in no real danger. And you also said if we are successful, it is worth one million dollars, and we would be attacking the bad guys."

"That's correct."

"In that case, count me in. But how did you get a working Tomahawk?"

"A combination of money and a promise to do something about those Muslim terrorists was all it took. You would be surprised at how many people hate those terrorists."

"But how about the nuclear warhead? I have no experience with those except sending it the signal to detonate. I will not be able to check out the warhead."

"We have someone with many years of experience who will work with you. Your only responsibility is with what you know, the Tomahawk."

Chapter 58

Chicago
Present Time

The large stockpile of money accumulated from the Mecca airline crash was used by Selah to buy an RDS-420 thermonuclear weapon from the Russian Mafia. This was an obsolete warhead slated for decommission that fell into the hands of the mafia. Only 14 of them were made, but the Russian mafia was willing to sell it because of the $150 million dollars, but more importantly, they believed in the cause of attacking radical Muslim terror. This was the same mafia group with which Major Sevorov had been associated.

Tactical nuclear weapons range from nuclear landmines and nuclear artillery shells to small warheads delivered by planes or missiles. The yields range from less that one-kiloton all the way up to about 1000 kilotons. They are designed to be used in battle situations against specific military targets such as very large concentrations of enemy forces. Tactical nuclear weapons are generally not the subject of arms control treaties and are not physically controlled by the sophisticated mechanisms employed for strategic weapons. As such, they represent an increasing danger of proliferation and of acquisition by terrorists. The old Soviet Union had about 20,000 of these tactical nuclear weapons, and these weapons were not all accounted for after the Soviet Union split up.

The Russian RDS-420 thermonuclear limited edition bomb has a low-fission 5-7 kiloton primary design. However, it has a pure thermonuclear secondary of about 52 kilotons. The beauty is that by both weight and volume, it should easily fit into the Tomahawk.

Chapter 59

Present Time

The vast desert spread out endlessly before them. The hard bumpy road jostled the cloth-covered truck that took them to the assembly building.

Saleh, Commander Miles, and Ivan Gurov had all flown in separately and met at the King Khalid International Airport which was located about 20 miles north of Riyadh, Saudi Arabia, so they did not have to go through the city, but headed east and then north towards their destination.

Their cover story was that they worked with an oil-reclaiming project to see if advance methods could improve the recovery in some of the declining oil fields.

Saleh was driving the truck the few hundred miles on the two-lane highway towards a small building he rented a bit north of the city of Ra's al Khafji.

Ra's al Khafji is in Saudi Arabia near the Persian Gulf, quite close to Kuwait. It was a perfect location for them. It is isolated with few nosey people anywhere around. It also is just across the Gulf from Iran and within 400 miles of the Iranian target they planned to destroy.

As a nuclear scientist Ivan could read English quite well, however he looked to be at least 60 years old and wore two of those large over-the-ear type hearing aids. Saleh quickly learned that he could understand if Saleh spoke loudly and slowly. When Ivan spoke it was in highly accented English, so communication was difficult, but possible.

"Look, a roadblock," said Ivan in a fearful and highly accented voice.

"Do not be concerned," replied Saleh. "Everything has been pre-arranged."

As promised, Saleh showed some papers to the Saudi soldiers, said a few words in Arabic, and they were on the way again. It was as if Saleh had very dedicated contacts in Saudi Arabia who thought of everything and smoothed the way.

It was immediately apparent that Ivan could understand English but thought in Russian and seemed to be unable to formulate his thoughts in a way that he could speak intelligible sentences. This was not unusual, since English is the scientific language, but reading it and not speaking it, is the norm.

"I want you to know that both of you are in the same situation. Ninety-five percent of both your pay depends on a successful explosion. You have to be a team and depend on each other. If one of you makes a mistake, then you both will have a bad payday. Additionally, we will be in much greater danger if the nuke doesn't explode, because then they will know it was a tomahawk and they will know its range and possible launch areas. If it explodes, all evidence will be destroyed and it could take weeks before they can even have a good guess."

It was mid-afternoon when they arrived at the old building that appeared to have once been a storage site for oil equipment. It was unkempt and in desperate need of paint and maintenance.

An armed guard carrying a British L24A1 assault rifle, stood near the building. Saleh got out of the truck, said something to the armed guard who smiled before getting into a nearby car, and left. Then Saleh opened the building's large garage door, started the electric generator, and they drove the truck into the building. As they drove in to the building, Commander Miles's jaw dropped. "I never expected to see such a well-equipped fabrication facility way out here and in such a dilapidated building," he said.

What Commander Miles saw was as modern and as high quality as any fully-equipped machine shop he had been to in America. There were hydraulic lifts, computers, and more tools than he knew what to do with. He saw Geiger counters, lead-lined aprons and gloves, just about everything needed to perform the simple tasks required for final assembly. "Only the best for our sensitive work," replied Saleh. "You should have more than enough here to make any necessary modifications. There are three iron cots already made up for sleeping in the back, a shower in the rest room, but I am afraid the food is only MRE's."

"What is that?" asked Ivan.

"It is the initials that stand for Meals Ready to Eat. It's military type food, but they are surprisingly good. I thought it would be enough, seeing as how we probably will be here only a day or two."

"The accommodations are fine," said Commander Miles. "So far everything has exceeded my expectations. When will the nuke and Tomahawk arrive?"

"See those crates in the corner? They are here now. Let's have a bite to eat, change clothes, and see what we have."

After dinner they opened the crates and found everything they needed. "It's been a long trip so let's turn in, get a good night's sleep, and get up early tomorrow and do it," said Saleh. There were no arguments.

Chapter 60

Present Time

The next morning there was no smell of bacon frying, but the MRE's were exceptional. They came from the U. S. and were head and shoulders above those things they called K-rations in Vietnam. Each meal had a hydrated calcium device that would heat the food when water was added, but the microwave that was thoughtfully included with the food worked much better.

One reason both Commander Miles and Ivan Gurov were needed was the connection between the nuke and the missile. The dimensions and weight were already determined to be compatible, but this warhead was never tested with this carrier. Another important reason is that Ivan was experienced and knew how to handle radioactive material, and in particular Russian nukes. Nuclear devices require a lot of maintenance because the radioactive material they use can wreak havoc on their electrical system. A complete set of spare parts came with the nuke, but Commander Miles would not know how to test and replace any damaged parts of the nuclear warhead.

By using the mil-spec GPS, highly sophisticated systems, and a raft of other top-secret technologies, the cruise missile can deliver a powerful offensive strike against the enemy. Commander Miles programmed the Tomahawk flight path to gain altitude over the Persian Gulf, and to remain very high so that there would be no problems crossing the Zagros Mountains.

This version of the Tomahawk has an inertial and terrain contour matching (TERCOM) guidance system and could be programmed to fly just above the ground, but Commander Miles thought this was more risky. The Tomahawk is a highly survivable weapon, and at high attitudes, radar detection is difficult because the missile has an extremely small cross-section. Also, infrared detection is difficult because the very small turbofan engine emits a low level of heat. Since Iran was not expecting a cruse missile, there was no risk of discovery, so it was agreed that the Tomahawk would fly at a high altitude until it descended to its burst height of about 2000 feet as it approached Qom.

As planned, the differences between the Russian and American systems were slight and the installation and connections were easily made. "I am slightly concerned about the age of the tritium," said Ivan. "It appears to be about one-and-a-half years old and not as active as it once was."

"What does that mean?"

"The fusion core is made up of a tritium-impregnated lithium-deuterium gas, also called heavy hydrogen. The tritium has to be bred in nuclear fission reactors and its half-life is only a little more than twelve years. This tritium has only lost a little of its strength. I could use the palladium filter that came with the nuke to remove the helium-three byproduct and thereby concentrate the tritium. But that would take a lot of time and this tritium is fresh enough to do a good job. The explosion may not be quite up to its maximum potential, but it will still be a very powerful thermo-nuclear explosion."

"That's good enough. I am not concerned with the chemical makeup or the absolute strength. I just want a thermonuclear explosion, so let's go with it." But Saleh thought it strange that Ivan, who could barely speak English, seemed to talk much better than before. Maybe it was the difference between talking about science and talking about yourself and your feelings.

By mid-afternoon everything was completed and the Tomahawk was programmed, armed, loaded in its launch tube, and in the firing position in the back of the truck with the canvas covering drawn down upon it. Even though the launch could happen immediately, the agreed time was at daybreak the next morning. At that time, few people would be awake and the bright plume of the rocket boosters during liftoff, and the glow from the Tomahawk jet engine, would be less visible during daylight.

Chapter 61

Present Time

The next morning, Saleh didn't need an alarm clock to wake up. He was very anxious to find out if these many months of work would result in a successful nuclear detonation on the correct target. He quickly woke the others and jumped in the makeshift shower.

As the faint light in the sky began to bring in this critical day, the cloth covered truck and its Tomahawk missile cargo left the assembly building. They drove for ten minutes to an even more secluded area near the Persian Gulf, parked, and looked around to be sure there were no spectators. Then they put on the emergency brakes and pulled up the truck's cloth cover. Would the missile take off properly? Would the warhead work? They would soon find out.

They rolled out the 200 feet of ignition wire and made the final connection to the battery. Then they all dropped to the ground and Commander Miles pushed the button to ignite the missile's solid-state booster.

Almost instantly an explosion of light erupted from the Tomahawk booster, immediately followed by a loud roar. The countryside lit up brightly from the flames. Within three seconds the missile lifted off, turned towards its target, and accelerated with amazing speed. In a very brief time, the extremely small turbofan jet engine took over from the booster and they saw the Tomahawk fly a mile or so into the Persian Gulf. Sleek, graceful and lethal, it was now a speck in the sky, and then they saw it no more.

The armed Tomahawk was on its way, approximately 400 miles, towards latitude 34.64528 and longitude of 50.88083, the city of Qom, Iran. At about 500 miles per hour, it would be there in slightly less than an hour.

Qom is the largest center for Shi'a Muslim scholarship and radical Muslim terror in the world. From 1958 until 1964, Ayatollah Ali Khomeini, who overthrew King Pahlavi, the Shaw of Iran, continued his studies in Islamic and terror in the seminary of Qom. Thousands of other radical Islamics and terror sponsors studied and graduated from the schools in Qom. This was indeed the center of radical Islam terror.

When one thinks about scholarship in Qom, one must remember that it is not the type of scholarship that most people think of. Students can graduate with a degree from the university simply by proving they can recite the entire Koran by heart. 'Koran' actually means recitation and to memorize the entire Koran is one of the highest honors in Muslim society. This may be because Muhammad himself was illiterate, so scholarship was never as important for Muslim as it is in the rest of the world.

But there was no time for Saleh and his group to reflect on this now. They drove the truck back to the fabrication facility and switched vehicles, driving away in the gray Lexus RX that was parked in the building.

"Shouldn't we have policed the building and wiped it down for fingerprints?" asked Commander Miles.

"No, that's not necessary. I hired the armed guard you saw when we arrived to remove the Tomahawk launch tube, the Geiger counter, and all other sensitive equipment and dump them in the Persian Gulf. Then he will bring in a few drums of gasoline and burn the building to the ground. It will look like it started from the truck's gas tank then spread to the stored gasoline, and be classified as an accident. That will remove any trace of us. Now all we have to do is get back to Riyadh and fly out. It will be days before anyone even starts to explore where the Qom nuke came from."

"Why days?"

"The story we will broadcast is that the nuke was planted in a building somewhere in the city of Qom. It will take a few days before they do the necessary science and figure out that it exploded at an altitude of about 2000 feet and not at ground level, and was probably a missile. Even then they will have no idea how, or from where, the missile came. Even if someone saw it coming from this direction, it still means it could have come from a ship in the Persian Gulf or some other country like Kuwait, Qatar, or Bahrain, to name a few."

"Still, I will be most happy to be on a plane out of here," said Ivan Gurov, in his extremely accented English. "As a matter of fact, I will not even begin to relax until the plane takes off."

"I'm with you," said Commander Miles.

"Don't worry. You will be at the airport in less than an hour, and your plane to London will leave about two hours after we arrive there. Everything, and I mean everything, has been taken care of. We even have tickets for your connecting flights from London. Relax," replied Saleh.

"I will take you to the airport, but I won't be flying with you today. My plane doesn't leave until late tomorrow. I have to take care of a few payments and many other things. Then I will be following you to London late tomorrow afternoon. By then, I am sure you will both be safely home."

182

Chapter 62

Qom, Iran
Present Time

The students finished their morning prayers and breakfast at the Shi'a radical Muslim university Howzeh-ye Elmieh. It was a perfectly beautiful mild morning with a bright rising sun and a cloudless, deep blue sky, so today class moved outside.

Ayatollah Ayyad began his daily teaching, "A martyr will have certain privileges with God. He is forgiven his sins on the shedding of the first drop of his blood. He is shown his place in paradise. A crown of glory is placed on his head. He will marry seventy-two virgins.

"Of course it is hard to leave our families, go to strange lands, meet interesting people and kill them. But it is our duty to be martyrs and to do just that. To kill an infidel is not murder; it is the path to Heaven. If we don't defend our religion, then who would do it? Can we ask the old people or the children to do it?

"We must aim to always fulfill the rules of God, and God wants us to give up our lives for jihad."

One of the students raised his hand and asked, "I know we should kill the unbelievers. You have taught us that they are no better than unclean cockroaches and they are manifestations of Satan. You have explained that Allah will destroy them, anyway, on the day of reckoning, and that he will rejoice at their suffering. But my question is, will it be acceptable to accidentally kill an innocent Muslim in our war with the devil unbelievers?"

Questions were rare since the prophet Muhammad taught that Allah hated questions, but this seemed to be a question that needed an answer.

Ayatollah Ayyad smiled and replied, "Of course it is absolutely acceptable. We have thoroughly researched this in the Koran and can report that everyone is in agreement. You can kill innocent bystanders without feeling guilt. God will identify those who deserve to die and send them to hell. The innocent who is hurt, he won't suffer. He becomes a martyr. An innocent Muslim killed in the cause of defending Islam will go straight to heaven.

"Just look at our holy Koran. In verse 3:169, it says "Think not of those who are slain in God's way as dead. Nay, they live finding their sustenance in the presence of their Lord." And in verse 4:101 it says, "For the unbelievers are unto you open enemies."

Just then the Ayatollah saw a bright flash and looked up. Thinking it was lighting he looked around and then there it was. But something was wrong. Instead of the blue flash from lightning this was orange and yellow. And there was something else. What looked like a huge tornado cloud was quickly forming about two miles away. The column of smoke in the strange tornado glowed red and yellow, and many colors in between. It grew and rose towards heaven.

The students had also turned and looked at the strange phenomenon. One of the students stood and said, "My God! It is a sign telling us what to do. It is a sign from Allah!"

The gamma rays from the blast, which travel at the speed of light, caused the Ayatollah and the students to feel rather strange and very hot.

The Ayatollah nodded and smiled, but shortly after he first saw the bright flash, a huge concentration of what seemed like the loudest noise he ever heard on earth surrounded him and penetrated his being down to his very core. He felt his body scorching hot, and the ear splitting sound brought pain to his head as the powerful shock wave threw him violently to the ground. His panicked expression during those last few moments said everything. Then the walls of the nearby school severely distorted, oscillated, and collapsed. Unseen neutrons and gamma rays irradiated everything. The Ayatollah died in that instant, and class was over.

Chapter 63

Riyadh, Saudi Arabia
Present Time

Saleh dropped Commander Miles and Ivan Gurov off at the King Khalid International Airport. They would embark on their flight to London in about approximately two hours. Saleh then continued past the airport and drove about thirty miles to the Al Faisaliah hotel located along the fashionable King Fahad Road in the capital city of Riyadh. This amazing city was built with oil money, and now has a population of over four million people. Due to its wealth, it has a higher quality of living than many cities, including Los Angeles and Miami.

The Al Faisaliah Hotel lobby was very crowded and noisy with many people arriving for a party, or some other apparently happy function, but Ahmed Yamamah, who Saleh was visiting, had a very spacious private apartment on the top floor of the hotel. Ahmed was a very high up official in the Saudi Arabian Ministry of Defense and Aviation.

It was Ahmed who started the T-3 group. Saleh had no idea whether this was actually condoned by the higher levels of the Saudi government or if Ahmed and his small group decided to initiate the plan by themselves. He did not even know if Ahmed even had a group at all, but he couldn't have done everything by himself. Whichever way, there was no doubt that Ahmed controlled a very large amount of money and he had many invaluable contacts in the Saudi government who could get things done.

Still, something in Saleh believed that the T-3 group was started, and secretly sanctioned, by the top levels of Saudi government. Iran is a Shiite country and Saudi Arabia is a Sunni country, and these two Muslim sects have been at war with each other for much of the last fourteen hundred years.

The elevator stopped at the top floor and Saleh knocked on Ahmed's door. "Enter, I have been expecting you," was the reply and Saleh put a big smile on his face, entered and hugged Ahmed.

"It's good to see you brother," said Saleh. They were not actual brothers, but good friends, and of course T-3 associates.

"Have we been successful?"

"I believe so, but we will have to wait and find out. Tell me, why Qom?"

"Most westerners mistakenly believe that Islamic terrorists are trying to take over their countries with bombs and hijacking. This is totally false. That violence is used to prove their power and dominance to other Muslims. The real goal of Islamic terrorists is to rebuild the grand caliphate, which is basically centralized Muslim control over all aspects of life. They want to destroy the Saudi Kingdom, then they can bring down the west by restricting the export of oil."

"Why do they want to destroy us?"

"To achieve their goal of destroying the west, they plan to first take over all Muslim countries, especially oil rich countries such as Saudi Arabia. Then, with the money and power of controlling the world's oil, they defeat the apostate regimes in the west. After that, they plan to destroy infidels globally, and then declare victory.

"Iran always had designs of taking over the Saudi Kingdom. After all, we have the key religious site of Mecca and all that Saudi oil. In November of 1979, they tried to ferment a revolution by seizing the Grand Mosque in Mecca with about 200-armed radical Islamic terrorists. Their goal was to start a revolt and overthrow the Saudi ruling family. Thousands of worshipers were taken hostage, resulting in many hundreds of them being killed. In total, there was far more damage and more deaths in 1979 than there was in the T-3 airplane Mecca attack.

"Our plan depends on the misdirection we created. Our attack on our own city of Mecca deeply planted the seeds of uncertainty on anyone who would accuse us of complacency on the attack on Iran.

"The group we work for are high ranking men who live in Saudi Arabia.

"As you know, most Muslims are ordinary, peace-loving people working on their own dreams and problems, but many of the world's more than forty-odd majority-Muslim countries have accepted Shari'a (strict Islamic law). Those that have not are under unrelenting pressure to do so. Hundreds of thousands of Muslims are killed every year in the struggle for religious political control and Shari'a. In Sudan alone the Muslim government has exterminated more than two million Sudanese.

"For an Islamic terrorist group to survive, it must be able to replace fallen recruits with fresh converts. The execution of successful operations helps to serve this purpose, but the recruits must believe that the mission is worth the sacrifices they make. If terrorist attacks result in counter-terrorist attacks against important Islamic targets, then the sacrifices are not worth it. When it is demonstrated that the long-term results are negative, terror will no longer offer a sense of empowerment. The morale within the group will sink, potential converts will dry up, and existing recruits will leave.

"There is a violent schism between the Shiite Muslims and us Sunnis. The split started in the seventh century with a fight over the Shiite belief that only the direct descendants of Muhammad could lead Islam. As you know, we thought that any worthy man could lead the faithful, even if they were not a relative of Muhammad. This quickly led to violence and we have been at war ever since. We are winning since about eighty-five percent of Muslims are Sunnis, but they keep fighting. Iran is a Shiite country and they want to take us over. Consequently, we always thought that we would nuke the radical Shiites."

"What? Then why did they have us attack Mecca? It's in Saudi Arabia."

"Yes, but one reason for choosing Mecca is to put all suspicion away from Saudi citizens. Also, they knew the plane would not do any lasting damage. But a nuke! That can't go off anywhere in Saudi Arabia. It has to go to Iran, and Qom is their center of radical teachings about terror.

"Additionally, the Russian mafia would not sell us the nuke until we proved to them we would use it against terror. Russia also has difficulty with the radical Muslims and they wanted to make sure we were not radical. We told them about the airplane and Mecca before it happened, so they trust us, but they will still sell us only one nuke at a time. They claim to have over twenty taken during the transition from the USSR and Russia, so we can get another, if we need it.

"But Mecca was the key and we got approval from an important official in the Saudi government. That's how we got the Saudi work visas, the seed money, and various help you weren't even aware of."

"OK. But why would the Saudis give that approval?"

"The reason we are working to neutralize the radicals is plain old fear. We know that the first goal of al-Qaeda and other extremists is to take over our country and run our lives, then they will withhold oil from the west and probably start a major war.

"Many Saudis are more afraid of the radical Muslims than you are. The Saudi Arabian government would be overthrown long before the radicals could take over the U.S. They are much more vulnerable, and they are very aware of that fact."

"Is that how we were able to get into Saudi Arabia to launch that missile?"

"Yes, but that is just the tip of the iceberg. They helped us all along. They got us the work visas for the one-way trip to Mecca. They made sure only one air marshal was on board, and much more."

"How is that possible? Are they part of the government?"

"Yes and no. It is kind of like the Iran-Contra affair, back in the old days of President Ronald Reagan. At that time the government employees illegally sold weapons to Iran, and used the profits to fund Nicaraguan anti-Communist rebels, called the Contras. It was a case of individuals in the government doing things secretly, without the actual support of the government."

"It's the same with my contacts in America and Saudi Arabia. The few who helped, like me, are sworn to secrecy. They work for their governments, but this was not part of the government. I guess you can say it is a shadow government. I believe they have the support of higher-ups, but we will never know."

Ahmed Al Yamamah had the hotel television on tuned to a news channel. The story about the earthquake was on the bottom scroll bar. Saleh said, "Look." Ahmed saw it and jumped up.

"That's money in the bank and the end of terrorism," exclaimed Ahmed. "That earthquake has to be the nuke. We have the radicals on the run now."

"How many oil futures did you buy this time?"

"Plenty. We now have a large enough war chest to mount many more attacks against the radical terrorists and their supporters. The day is fast approaching when the killing of civilians to further radical religious beliefs will come to an end."

"Al-Qaeda and other radical Muslims are not in the least bit deterred by the huge nuclear weapon stockpile in the free world because they know it would not be used. But the T-3 group is a different story. We proved that we are a non-state entity with nuclear warheads poised to inflict massive nuclear destruction at targets in Iran and other radical Muslim targets. They know we will use them. So, now we are a credible deterrent. And how does a group such as Al-

Qaeda explain to the 'street' that they are responsible for another nuclear detonation?"

Chapter 64

Various locations
Present Time

Karen sat in her Paris hotel room and had the television and the radio both tuned to twenty-four hour news programs. The initial word of the attack on Qom erroneously presumed that either there was an earthquake or that Iran had detonated some kind of nuclear test. The indication from seismograph equipment indicated the epicenter was near a populated area, so it was probable that the event was an earthquake. Various broadcast networks reported it as an earthquake and added that they were trying to get more information of any damage.

When Karen heard this she let out an involuntary shout of victory. To celebrate she popped a bottle of French champagne and poured herself a glass. She drank it with a smile on her face and then grabbed her laptop and hurried out to a different hotel to send her already prepared e-mails to the various news media.

Commander Miles and Ivan Gurov separately cleared customs and walked through London's Heathrow airport. While they waited for their connecting flights to New York and Moscow respectively, the waiting room televisions broke in with a stunning announcement. NBC was the first station to read and understand Karen's e-mail.

"We just received word that the earthquake in Iran was not an earthquake, but was a nuclear explosion. We received an e-mail claiming credit for this attack. We are checking with the Iranian government to determine the truth. Phone calls made to the city of Qom do not go through, and television and radio broadcasts from Qom are off the air. We will report the results the moment we get them. Now back to our regularly scheduled program."

Commander Miles and Ivan Gurov could barely control their exuberance, but played it cool. Separately, they stopped at an airport lounge and sat across the room from each other. Commander Miles raised his Guinness Stout, Ivan raised his vodka, and silently they toasted each other.

Less than ten minutes later the NBC News announcer broke in again. "The nuclear blast has been confirmed. The North American

Aerospace Defense Command said that it did register a nuclear detonation in Iran and they are triangulating readings to determine the exact location. However it appears that the earthquake in Qom, Iran is connected to this detonation. We will break in again as soon as we get more information about what is going on."

Chapter 65

Various locations
Present Time

The blast from a 52 kiloton nuclear weapon is equal to the force of about 52,000 tons of TNT. When detonated a couple of thousand feet above the ground, it killed every exposed person within a radius of a mile and a half. The pressure wave destroyed or severely damaged all structures within a two mile radius of ground zero. Intense heat from the blast ignited mass fires resulting in third degree burns across the city.

This blast, although small by modern weapon comparison, was larger that the 1945 blast over Hiroshima that practically destroyed the city. The destruction of life and property in Qom by this "H" bomb was much greater.

The entire world was in shock. The nuclear genie was loose and out of the bottle and no one knew what this meant for the future.

Just as in the Mecca attack with the airplane, oil spiked and the equity markets crashed. And just like before, the T-3 group that knew in advance of the attack made huge amounts of money on oil futures.

But this time there was a major difference. The Arab streets did not react in the same way. Instead they seemed depressed and were almost silent. The power and magnitude and devastation of the attack did not permit cries of vengeance. Instead it brought an out crying of grief. This was a totally unexpected event, and the enormity of its power overwhelmed any response. What had God brought upon the true believers and why? The infidels should die in the fire and not the true believers. It seemed like the infidels had won. Something was wrong. But what was happening?

The world immediately began to organize relief measures. Rescue crews from almost every country that had them were dispatched to Qom. They were told to keep upwind from Qom, but it was still exceedingly dangerous. With the exception of those few who had "moon suits," the radiation kept them from approaching very close to ground zero.

The vast majority of people who die in a nuclear blast do not die in the explosion itself. Those within a few miles of ground zero are quickly vaporized or die from the blast, firestorm, or heat. Eventually, most fatalities come from radiation sickness caused by the high radiation dose received many miles from the blast.

The destruction was unbelievable. It was a throwback to the carnage of Hiroshima and Nagasaki during World War II. It was surrealistic, and every news media was transfixed and reported on almost nothing else. The death, the suffering, the radiation, it was totally unlike anything modern man had any recollection of since the nukes that ended World War II. For the entire world, it was a look into Hell.

After the tremendous nuclear explosion, people fled in all directions away from ground zero. They drove, walked or were carried to aid station positions far away from the radiation.

Many of the injured were almost unrecognizable. Their skin hung loosely from their chins. Their faces were red and so swollen that you could hardly recognize their features. Many of those not directly injured by the explosion were still exposed to dangerous doses of radiation during the subsequent fallout of radioactive particles. Anyone who received more than 500 rads would certainly get various diseases, hair loss, eye damage, leukemia and many other types of deadly cancer. Death and disfigurement would be the unbearable result.

A science expert explained the details of possible radiation doses. It sounded confusing as he spoke about doses of roentgens, called rems, per hour. He went on and on. "Converting this measurement to the work of Rolf Sievert, we divide the roentgens by about 100 to get the dosage in sieverts and find that there could be another 600,000 people killed or injured just by the radiation from the fallout. The injured people will include those who, many years later, develop cancer or become unable to have normal children because of the collective dose of radiation. It is therefore imperative that all people under the fallout path evacuate to a safe location, as rapidly as possible to minimize their exposure.

"There are many types of radiation sickness and symptoms caused by nuclear warfare. To minimize exposure, people should remain indoors until evacuated. They should not eat or drink anything that may have been radiated. Care centers in safe areas away from the fallout are now being set up and staffed by physicians from around the world.

"Calculating the reference dose rate and the decay curves it is possible to estimate the actual dose rate at any time after the fallout is complete. Complete measurements will be taken and risk calculations distributed.

"Drugs used as medical countermeasures for the prevention of acute radiation syndrome will be given to the first responders and remediators entering the contaminated areas.

Al-Jazeera, the Arab news organization reports:

Abu al-Zawahri, in a televised speech to westerners, said "Qom was proof that you work for the devil. Your rejection of Islam as the only way of life accepted by Allah puts you at great risk. This is your problem and you have to choose yourself. You have to realize that we Muslims are a nation of patience and endurance. We can suffer the injustice of nuclear war without flinching. All mankind needs to hunt down these abdominal terrorists. We will always stand firm to fight you with Allah's help until the coming of doomsday, which does not appear to be very far away."

Hour after hour, the horrendous news continued to monopolize the news. In the past, during World War II, there never was an international media to cover a story this big. This was the most important story of the twenty-first century.

Chapter 66

Various locations
Present Time

Shortly before the time of the nuclear detonation, Karen had sent her teaser e-mail to her pre-selected contact list. The e-mail just advised the various news media to stay tuned for the big story she would send them tomorrow. It was signed the T-3 group. This time the news reporters were waiting by their computers to get the next T-3 e-mail as soon as it came over the wire.

Finally, it came and various news media translated it from French and reported Karen's e-mail:

"The following e-mail message is from group T-3 that was responsible for the suicide attack on Mecca and claims responsibility for the nuclear attack on Iran."

"We are not willing to surrender our freedom and our religion to radical Muslims. We are prepared and willing to take their lives to preserve our freedom. Our motto is 'give me freedom or give you death,' and when we give you death, we do things in a very big way.

"Terrorism is targeting civilians to spread terror. We know that Mohammad killed civilians and kept captured women and children as slaves, but this is not the seventh century and if you continue this barbaric behavior you will burn. You will all burn.

"We have no problem if you attack military targets, but if you attack civilians we will attack your civilians and your "holy" places. We know that it is extremely important to you to keep these "holy" places pure and free of non-Muslims. But, unless you change your ways, you won't keep them free of radiation. Civilized countries cannot respond to terrorism effectively. Civilized countries are unwilling to do this, but we are not.

"We now possess the ultimate weapon with the power to destroy many innocent lives and do incalculable damage. It will lead to the total extinction of life in Iran.

"You Muslim terrorists go ahead and attack any target you want. But if you do, we will just say bye-bye baby. We don't give a damn. We don't believe in your BS and religious wars. They are stupid, and if you don't stop your stupid religious junk you will be totally destroyed. Nuke is God! Hey man, go ahead and make our day! We will explain to you what real terror is. Have you ever seen a Muslim die of radioactive sickness? We are talking about radioactive Mecca. You will see the nuclear light.

"It is the duty of all Muslims to do whatever is necessary to stop terrorists from attacking us infidels or all Islam's sacred sites will be destroyed. We are your worst nightmare, and you are the only hope of Islam.

"You mothers, fathers, and friends of terrorists hear me now. Your acts of terror will bring the nuclear destruction of your religious icons like Mecca, Medina, and others. You will not be able to go on your pilgrimage because there will just be an empty radioactive zone left to visit. Your terror against civilians will be totally responsible for our reaction. Stop your brutal terrorists and you can save these religious icons. It's up to you!

"All Muslims who want to save their holy sites must protest against terrorism committed in the name of religion. Muslims are required to take to the streets to protest when civilians are killed in the name of Islam. True Muslims must be brave and risk their lives to bring a truce and avoid more nuclear attacks.

"You should know that no enemy, no matter how civilized, compassionate and peaceful, should be taken lightly. But you thought our Atheistic compassion was weakness, and on 9/11, you woke the sleeping tiger.

"It appears that the governments of the western democracies are incapable of winning a long war against terrorists who reject the Geneva Convention rules. Under these rules, soldiers who fight out of uniform or commit atrocities such as murder prisoners or target and kill non-combatants may be shot by firing squads. During World War II, we did not hesitate to execute out of uniform saboteurs and spies.

"When the free countries tried to confront you in combat you hid in caves and holes in the ground. You wore civilian clothing to blend in with the larger population and pretended to be innocents. Yet when you attacked us you purposely attacked our civilians. You are cowards who will not openly face our armies.

"We want to be your friends. We abhor the killing of civilians, but you will not listen. If an opportunity for peace were to present itself, we would quickly take advantage of it, but you do not want peace. Instead you continue to use terrorist tactics against our innocents and children.

"If we have everything, but no freedom of belief and free choice of religion, we have nothing. If we have nothing, but freedom, we have everything and you have radioactivity.

"Our love of freedom is greater than your desire to push your radical religion upon us. You have forced us to use your own barbaric tactics to defend ourselves. You give us no choice but to fight fire with fire. Mecca and Qom are just the beginning. We know who you are. We know who your teachers are. We know where your holy terror sights are. And you do not know who we are or where we are located, or how to attack us. You do not know our resolve or what we are truly capable of doing. But we know exactly how to pound your false religious beliefs into fire and dust.

"In Mecca, your radical terrorists thought that we would just fly a plane into another target. They had no expectation that we would follow up with a nuclear attack. They were caught completely unaware. They completely underestimated our resolve and power, and they still do.

"Some will ask why we used nuclear weapons. They were on the market and we were forced to outbid a radical Muslim non-state player to keep them from getting these weapons. We know they would use them and, unless these groups are brought to task, they will eventually buy nukes elsewhere. Demonstrating their power in the hometown of their radical headquarters might affect their desire to buy more nukes. And our use of these weapons, in the long run, will save many lives if this madness persists.

"Have no doubt in your mind; we have many more nuclear weapons in our arsenal. They all have your name on them and you know by now we are entirely unafraid to use them. We are the first non-national nuclear superpower and as we proved, we are willing to use them. As a matter of fact, we are the ninth largest nuclear power in the world.

"You have mistaken our kindness, our civilization, and our softness for weakness. But we can change, like the water in the rock. When our emotions freeze, we split the rock apart.

"You know we have already attacked Mecca. You know we now have nukes. You do not know who we are so you cannot retaliate. We can destroy you, but you cannot harm us. We promise you that we will answer your terror with nuclear destruction of your shrines such as Mecca, Median, and others, and Mecca will take ten-thousand years to recover from the deadly radiation of a nuke. We are not Muslims and don't give one damn about your sites. We ourselves don't have any special sites for you to retaliate against.

"Radical Muslim terror will be responsible for the devastation of Islam's most precious sites. If you allow Muslim terror to flourish, the destruction will be your fault, your fault and only your fault!

"We are working on plans for the next attack. We have already pre-placed many weapons at various sites important to you. They are just waiting for one of our atheist martyr teams to arm and detonate them. And if you continue to attack free people we will detonate many at the same time just as you terrorists like to do. Next time we will detonate them simultaneously, in different locations.

"Our thousands of well-trained freedom teams will continue to destroy terrorists' headquarters until the moderate Muslims are willing to convince radical Muslims to cease and desist terror operations. Moderate Muslims must reject terrorism because it will harm Islam and destroy your religious sites. We cannot say it often enough. We will destroy your religious sites forever!

"Send us your treaty with a declaration of peace and we will honor it, as long as you also honor it. We will rest now while we await your reply. But if there is no reply, we will only rest for a short time before we go back to work. That's it. The ball is in your court. Respond or watch your religious junk destroyed.

"The hypocrisy and moral decay of Islamic terror against civilians will lead to the brutal humiliation of all Muslims by a superior nuclear force. We have the ninth largest nuclear arsenal and we are happy to use it against the evil devils who attack innocent civilians. You will die by the millions and we will celebrate your death. Your only hope is to turn in the radical terrorists to government authorities before they commit their criminal acts and cause your complete destruction.

"The great advantage we have over you scumbag radical Muslim terrorists is that we have a target rich environment with many possibilities of attack. In contrast, you Muslims do not know who we are or where to attack us. We are an extended very lethal network. We operate entirely outside the chain of command of any government or known group. We are totally flexible and entirely insulated from any political pressures including moral codes, methods, and timetables. None of our thousands of members know more that one other member and even their real identities are kept secret.

"Terrorists have a list of the targets they want to attack. We also have an extensive list of targets we will nuke. Yes, they are Muslim holy sites and radical Muslim learning centers. Radical Muslims will be completely responsible for their destruction. The list is our secret but you can probably guess what is on it. Come on, make our day. Attack something else and we will feel proud to destroy everything you hold dear. By the way, you may want to skip next year's trip to Mecca and Medina, and for safety's sake, don't travel anywhere in Iran or Saudi Arabia.

"Open your eyes, man. We have the means and, by God, the heart to destroy everything you hold dear. Let it end here or get ready to grieve much more. We hate you camel breath monsters and are very happy to kill you all to keep you from breeding.

"The bottom line is that you do not know who we are, but we know exactly who you are. We have the address of your headquarters. It is said that you should never threaten in public and you should never threaten something you cannot do. Well, we can do a lot – including many more nukes! Believe it!"

Chapter 67

Various locations
Present Time

The reaction of the world community to the T-3 tirade was complete shock. Every country on earth was quick to denounce the terror. But it was very real and no denunciation could change the radioactive sickness that plagued Iran and threatened to plague other important Muslim sites. This was, by no means, an empty gesture. This was for real, and it doesn't get any more real.

The residue samples collected from the Qom detonation site were sent to the Los Alamos National Laboratory where they were probed by an assortment of equipment including their gamma-ray spectrometer. The comparative strength of the various gamma radiation frequencies showed up as visual energy lines on the printout. This determined the proportions of the various elements that were in the nuclear devise. This would indicate where the ingredients of the bomb came from.

The resulting readouts of the various isotopes of uranium and plutonium plus traces of curium, neptunium, tritium, gadolinium, etc., gives the signature that tells the country of origin of the bomb. In this case, there was on doubt about the origin. It came from the old Soviet Union, or modern day Russia.

CNBC reports: "Dow Jones stocks have fallen 3,750 points since the Iran attack. The genie is out of the bottle, it cannot be returned; nuclear terror is here to stay, like it or not. Previously, the only nuclear bombs exploded in anger were ordered by President Truman over Hiroshima and Nagasaki, way back in 1945.

"It is well-known that Iran has used various proxies, such as the terror group Hamus, to do its dirty work throughout the world. By contrast, the T-3 group is apparently not a proxy of any country. As such, it is many times scarier. Instead of a nation behind them, this small-unknown group has somehow gathered the resources to become a first class nuclear power and a threat to the peace of the world. International law enforcement still has no idea who this group is or where it came from."

In Tehran, the capital of Iran, the radical Muslim spokesman, Mohammad Fazlullah, denied the Howzeh-ye Elmieh cleric's involvement in any terror, saying, "We want peace in the region and only want to offer Islamic law, as Prophet Muhammad, peace be upon him, said we should."

Mohammad Fazlullah is a graduate of the Howzeh-ye Elmieh university in Qom. He is with the Movement for the Enforcement of Islamic Law, a militant group which sent many hundreds of volunteers to fight in Afghanistan during the U.S. "occupation" in 2008.

"But speaking for our group, we want peace. We do not want any more nuclear bombs on Islamic soil. We will do everything we can to prevent nuclear terrorism." Thus began a growing Arab revulsion of al-Qaeda's, and similar group's, indiscriminate violence and thuggish behavior that threatens the very framework of Islam's most sacred sites.

The Iran Caliphate, which are the Islamic religious leaders, decided they needed peace, and they wanted it now before more nuclear weapons were detonated. They put out the word to all their proxy militia units, such as Hamus, to immediately cease all attacks.

The New York Evening Herald reports:

Muslim Leader Calls for an End of Terror

Abdul Abbas, one of the most respected Islamic leaders, called on militants to stop their useless attacks on western countries. His remarks came just a week after the nuclear attack in Iran.

He said that it is required of every Muslim to visit Mecca at least once in their lifetime. The possibility of it being destroyed by nuclear weapons is totally unacceptable. "I implore each and every one of you to report any attempted terrorist activities to the authorities," he said.

Mr. Abbas urged the militants to refrain from further attacks saying they were counterproductive. "This is not the time for this kind of act," he said. "Do not give the infidels more reason to attack our most sacred holy sites."

Chapter 68

Chicago
Present Time

Karen and Saleh met in the parking lot of the Museum of Science and Industry near 57th Street and Lake Michigan. This meeting would debrief Karen and talk about the next phase of the operation. They walked north until they came to a small, man-made pond where a few people were playing with radio-controlled toy boats and sat on a bench.

As they watched the toy boats, Saleh spoke. "Even a dangerous animal can be made harmless by re moving its claws and teeth. The teeth of the martyred terrorists are the approval of their social pears. Nuclear destruction in revenge of terror will quickly put a stop to their appeal and illusion of victory.

"We can only win this war if we are willing to detach ourselves from normal civilized principles and fight the dirty war of the radical Muslims. In this war nice guys don't finish first."

"I can't do this anymore," intruded Karen. "I can keep this a secret forever, but I just can't do it again!"

Saleh's face remained steadfastly impassive and there was a long silence. It was long enough to make Karen think that perhaps Saleh was not going to respond to her statement. But, finally he did.

He seemed confused and said, "What do you mean?" Saleh watched a tear running down Karen's face, stopping on her upper lip. "I want to know why you are talking this way."

"Why, for God's sake, did we kill of all those innocent people? I didn't know it would effect me this way, but it has," exclaimed Karen. "I just can't do this anymore. I just have second thoughts about using nuclear weapons."

Saleh struggled to contain his frustration and keep his composure. "I know just how you feel," he calmly replied.

Karen thought to herself that this was just a stock reply and Saleh had no idea how she really felt. He appeared to be quite pleased with the results and Karen already knew that he was very logical, but missing a whole lot in the feeling department.

"You know that it's for the better good," added Saleh. "Over a number of years the terrorists would kill many millions more people than died from the nuke. It was the same when those Japanese cities were nuked during the Second World War. The total of the Allies and Japanese killed would have been many times greater if there were no nukes."

"Paul Tibbets, who piloted the B-29 bomber Enola Gay that dropped the atomic bomb on Hiroshima, died at the ripe old age of 92. To his dying day, he insisted that he had absolutely no regrets about the mission and slept just fine at night."

"That's probably true. I know that the terrorists want to convert us or kill us. I know we have to fight back. But nuclear weapons, the carnage of so many innocent people, I can't do it anymore. I want to resign from this job. I just can't be a part of this carnage anymore."

Saleh shrugged, and then his eyes narrowed. "Karen you are out! After today we will have no more communication with you. However, I want to be completely sure you understand what I am saying. You will not mention T-3, or your role in it, to anyone. If you do, you will be eliminated. I hope you understand my meaning. Eliminated!

"Any allegations made against T-3 or against me will not stick. I have many alibis and you know next to nothing about T-3. But if you turn towards the dark side and fink on us, you personally, will not survive!

"Additionally, we will not permit you to suddenly start spending a lot of money. Keep almost all of your money in that secret Zurich numbered bank account you like and wait at least two years before you buy anything of significance. Do you understand and agree?"

"Oh, yes! I guarantee you don't have to worry about me. I give you my word. I will not do anything that calls attention to myself.

"It's amazing. I was part of a major turning point in history and I can never tell anyone. I brought peace to the world and if they only knew they would put me in jail for a thousand years. My God, it's amazing."

Epilogue

So what will come about as a result of the nuclear explosion that occurred? Some say that the genie was let out of the bottle and the world will destroy itself.

Others think that the infidel nations of the west have over 80,000 thermonuclear weapons and the Muslim countries have just a few. The result will be the complete destruction of Islam.

Saleh likes to think that the advent of thermonuclear weapons, detonated by a small group of anti-terrorists, was a watershed experience and we will never go back to the way things were.

He believes that years from now, historians will look back and see our actions as a turning point. They will say that we changed history. There will now be room for all religions. He hopes that this will finally bring peace to a world that never knew it.

Addendum

As a proofreader and editor, I find this work to be a very important piece of literature and of the utmost relevance. While this novel is not an indictment of any particular race, religion or ethnicity, it certainly serves as a wake up to how serious the issue of terrorism has become in our world.

My involvement in this project has been the result of wishing to see the world around me educated and prepared for the worst possible scenarios in existence. The authors need to be commended and this work shared with as many of your loved ones and acquaintances as possible.

I pray we would all do our parts.

G. Stephens, editor
Puppetmaster@hushmail.com

Printed in the United States
140619LV00005B/33/P